The Cave
of the Inca Rey

by Jeanette Windle

ACE *Publications*

The Cave of the Inca Rey
by Jeanette Windle

Cover illustration by Marie Tabler
Copy Editor: Julia C. Hansen
Book design by Amy Haynes
Proofreaders: Anita Nish and Sally Bradley

Published by
PACE *Publications*
PO Box 1982
Independence, MO 64055

Formerly published in a trilogy form as
Adventures in South America
by Multnomah Youth, Sisters, Oregon
(Now out of print)

Printed in the United States of America
Set in Times New Roman 12 point
ISBN 0-918407-11-7

To Melody Hobbs
my first and most loyal fan

Contents

A Desperate Decision

$\mathcal{G}$listening white in the silver light of a full moon, the massive stone walls of the ancient Indian city loomed ahead of the running children. Shouts of anger behind them told the pair that their escape had been discovered. Feeling like their lungs would burst, the two panting children ran along the outer wall of the main temple complex.

Pulling his sister to a halt at the foot of a narrow stone staircase, Justin peered around the crumbling blocks of stone carved by Inca craftsmen centuries ago. He jumped back as he caught sight of two shadowy figures running along the high wire fence that encircled the complex.

The clang of a metal-tipped boot echoed across the rough ground as one of the figures, a bulky outline against the shimmering dust of the stars, stumbled and fell against a dark boulder. Cursing, he jumped to his feet. A moment later, a bright finger of light from an electric lantern probed the darkness behind the children.

"Come on, Jenny!" Justin hissed. He pushed his sister up

the narrow steps that opened onto a vast courtyard. Dodging between the giant stone figures—tokens of long-past conquered nations—that dotted the open courtyard, the two children made their way toward the main entrance.

Suddenly both children started with fear as a strangely high, thin voice echoed, seemingly inches away. Then they relaxed as they remembered the stone "loudspeaker" across the court where Inca priests had addressed the crowds that once filled this temple. Hidden behind a featureless granite figure, the children looked up anxiously at the wide-open grass strip that lay between them and safety.

A wispy cloud skittered across the face of the pale-gold ball above them. Taking advantage of the sudden shadow, Justin grabbed his sister's hand and yanked her across the open ground, and then through a wide, crumbled opening that had once been a door.

It was not a *real* door; it was just two weathered granite blocks on either side of a wide opening. A third stone block balanced on top of the other two to form a square entryway. Here, feather-caped warriors glistening with gold ornaments had guarded the temple hundreds of years ago.

A sudden cold beam of light told them their pursuers were again close behind. Holding hands, the two children sprinted for open fields beyond the courtyard, but Jenny stumbled and fell, her sudden cry alerting the men behind them. They froze for a moment, hoping no one had heard Jenny's cry. But seconds later they heard running feet.

Justin pulled Jenny to her feet. Reluctantly turning away from the open fields, the two children jumped over a shallow ditch the short rainy season had dug in the sandy soil. A solitary, evenly shaped hill lay before them. When they reached the base of the mound, no one was in sight. "I think we can slow down now," Justin wheezed.

But just as he spoke, a large, bulky figure rose from behind a jumbled pile of stone blocks only yards away. The white-gold rays of the full moon showed a cruel face smiling triumphantly.

"We've got you now," their massive pursuer gloated hoarsely. Justin glanced back toward the ruins. A short, skinny man walked unhurriedly toward the pair cowering against the hillside.

Justin tapped his sister on the shoulder. "Come on!" he whispered. Taking their would-be captors by surprise, the two children turned and quickly climbed the steep side of the mound. The two men went after them with hoarse, angry shouts, but the children had the head start they needed.

Above them, a large opening in the face of the hill had been sealed shut with cement bricks. Heavy boulders had been piled against the bricks as added insurance against intruders, but at one side a dark, ragged-looking area above the heaped-up boulders showed where a few bricks had crumbled away. Justin scrambled toward that spot.

When Jenny realized where he was going, she hesitated. "We can't go in there! We'll be killed!"

Justin was already squeezing through the small opening. "Yes, we can. God will protect us. Besides, there's nowhere else to go!"

He pulled his sister through the narrow hole, and the two of them backed into the darkness as a long arm reached in and groped for them. The men swore loudly. The opening was too small for either of them. They kicked against the bricks, but the solid wall resisted their kicking and pounding.

Jenny and Justin leaned against the stone wall of the cave, their chests on fire from the violent exercise. They hugged their thin jackets close to ward off the intense cold, and Justin remembered that this plateau sat at thirteen thousand feet— well over two miles above sea level. When they had climbed down from the airplane only a few days ago, they had gasped for breath after simply walking across the airport.

It was now quiet outside. The cave was pitch black, except for the faint moon-glow that shone through the opening. Anything could be hiding in that blackness, they knew. His arm around Jenny, Justin shut his eyes and tried to think.

How in the world did we get into this mess? he wondered desperately.

Chapter 1

An Unexpected Visitor

A sudden bang echoed through the one-story, cream-colored house as the kitchen door slammed hard. Mrs. Parker glanced up from the head of lettuce she was washing, frowning at the noise. "Justin Parker!"

The tall, husky thirteen-year-old flushed to the roots of his short-cropped red hair, and turned to shut the door again— more quietly this time. He knew his mother's strict rule against slamming doors. He paused a moment to breathe in the sweet, spicy fragrance coming from the oven, then threw a well-worn bat and baseball glove into the corner by the door. Tossing an equally well-used baseball up and down in one hand, he joined his mother at the sink.

"Mom!" he growled, his eyes stormy with annoyance, "you've got to keep Jenny out of my hair!"

Mrs. Parker moved to a wide work island in the center of the kitchen. Before she could answer, the door slammed again. A slim girl rushed into the kitchen. She too carried a baseball glove. Tossing it after her brother's, she leaned on the counter and pushed back heavy, dark curls that were slightly damp from her running. Her golden eyes flashed fire.

"Mom, you've got to stop Justin from being so mean to me!"

Reaching for a small knife, Mrs. Parker, an older version of Jenny, calmly began slicing a tomato into a large wooden salad bowl. She didn't seem at all surprised at the storm.

"Why, I thought you two were the best of friends today. What happened?"

Before Jenny could open her mouth, Justin complained, "It's Jenny, Mom! You've got to keep her away when I'm playing ball with the boys. It's embarrassing! None of the other guys' sisters tag along!"

Jenny lifted an unapologetic chin and said huffily, "You know I can play better than any of them!"

There was truth in her words. Only a few minutes younger than Justin, his twin sister, Jenny, was as tall as he and a forward on her seventh-grade basketball team. She loved sports as much as she did books. Though so much like her easygoing mother in looks, Jenny seemed to move through life at a gallop.

At the moment, her height ran to long, slim arms and legs, but Jenny didn't have the awkwardness of many lanky girls. As she had said, she could beat most of the boys in the neighborhood in a foot-race or a baseball game.

Justin provided a good balance to the up-and-down moods of his sister. Calm and even-tempered most of the time, he had a stubborn streak that kept him from being pushed around. His steady, hazel eyes noticed everything that went on around him, and he liked to think things through before talking.

Jenny, on the other hand, let everyone know exactly what she was thinking. "Justin used to like playing ball with me," she continued, now in a sadder tone.

"That was different!" Justin replied with exasperation. "The guys don't like girls hanging around during a ball game! I get teased about having Jenny along. You understand, don't you, Mom?"

Mrs. Parker sighed and laid her chopping knife beside the wooden salad bowl. Putting an arm around her angry daughter's shoulders, she said, "Jenny, there are times when boys like to play on their own without girls. You wouldn't like Justin tagging along all the time when you're playing with your girl friends, would you?"

"But that's the problem, Mom!" Sudden tears brimmed in Jenny's golden-brown eyes. "I don't have any girl friends now that school is out. There aren't any girls my age in the neighborhood—just boys! The only time I see my friends is in Sunday school. I get so bored playing by myself all the time while Justin is out having fun with the boys. It's not fair! Why should they mind me playing?"

Mrs. Parker cracked the door of the oven and inspected its contents, then lifted two pies onto the counter.

"Jenny, I'm sorry you don't have any friends close by, but you need to be more understanding of your brother. Let him spend some time alone with his friends. As for you, Justin, try to be more patient with your sister. It's hard for her this summer."

Her stern eye caught theirs, and they reluctantly nodded their heads. Justin stiffled a grin as he glanced at his sister. Being twins, Justin and Jenny had always been the best of friends.

"I have to admit, she really is the best catcher in the neighborhood, Mom." The grin spread across his freckled face. "You should have seen her! She grabbed a pop fly ball and got Danny Olson out just as he slid into home plate. I guess that's why the guys were so mad. If she'd miss occasionally, they'd think she was okay."

An answering smile banished the tears from Jenny's eyes. "I'm sorry I teased you so much," she told her brother sincerely.

"Yeah, well, I'm sorry I yelled," Justin growled back. Apologies embarrassed him. "I don't mind you playing with us, but . . . the guys don't see it that way. Hey, the game's probably over by now anyway. Want to play catch until supper?"

Harmony restored, Justin gave his mother a hard hug, then collected his baseball equipment. Jenny added a quick kiss, then picked up her glove from the corner. Leaning over her mother's shoulder, she sniffed and inspected the two pies, oozing dark-red through slits in the top crust.

"Ummm, cherry pie! What's the special occasion, Mom?"

"Oh, didn't I mention it?" her mother answered. "We're having company for supper."

"Company? Who is it, Mom?"

Mrs. Parker swatted Justin's fingers with a pot holder as he reached for a dangling edge of golden crust. "I thought I'd keep that a secret for now," she said with a straight face.

"Aw, Mom!" the twins groaned in unison. "Come on, tell us!" Jenny added.

Their mother gave an exaggerated sigh. She knew she would have no peace until she told them, but she enjoyed teasing her two lively children once in a while. "Okay, I'll give you one hint. Your father just left for SeaTac airport."

"Uncle Pete!" the two chorused.

Seeing the smile that crept into her mother's eyes in spite of her attempts to look innocent, Jenny threw her arms around her mom. "We're right, aren't we?" she asked. Mrs. Parker nodded. "Yippee!"

Pete Parker, their father's brother, was Justin and Jenny's favorite uncle. A widower with no children, he was an executive of Triton Oil, a large oil company. He spent much of his time jetting around the world, troubleshooting for the company in different countries. Whenever he had free time, often at an hour's notice, he would fly into Seattle where his brother Ron worked as a computer analyst for Boeing.

The children were used to Uncle Pete's sudden appearances and had a large collection of "treasures" he had brought them from all corners of the world. Like the twins' parents, Uncle Pete was a dedicated Christian. His special interest was missions, and he often visited missionaries in different countries while he was there on business. Jenny and Justin loved the stories he told of the strange and wonderful things that happened when these missionaries told people about Jesus.

Mrs. Parker smiled at her children's exuberance. "Okay, kids, you got what you wanted. Now get on out of here and give me some peace and quiet! Jenny, I need to have you back here in half an hour to set the table. Justin, it's your turn to do dishes.

"And put away your junk when you're done with it," she called out the screen door to their rapidly retreating backs. "I don't want to find it all over the yard!"

Justin had just scrambled over the fence to recover a missed ball when he heard the distinct rumble of his father's station wagon.

"Come on, Jenny. They're here!" he shouted, vaulting back

over the fence. He tossed the ball and glove onto the front steps, but, remembering his mother's plea, he picked them up again. Together they quickly stored the baseball equipment in its proper place in the garage.

By the time they had finished, their father had already pulled their dark-green station wagon into the garage and was stepping out of the driver's seat. Jenny threw herself into her tall, lanky father's arms. Upon meeting Mr. Parker, it was obvious to people how Justin came to have red hair and hazel eyes!

Ron Parker enthusiastically lifted his daughter from the floor and whirled her around. If Justin had inherited his coloring, it was Jenny who shared his outgoing personality.

"Hey, don't I get a hug, too?" Like his brother, Uncle Pete was tall and red-headed, but he was much broader. A full red beard made him look like a youthful Santa Claus. Slapping his well-rounded front, he liked to blame his size on the hospitality he couldn't refuse in the many countries he visited.

After greeting his nephew and niece, Uncle Pete reached into the back seat and pulled out the one small suitcase that was all he ever carried. "Something smells mighty good in your mother's kitchen," he declared. "Let's go eat, kids. I'm starved!"

Gathered around the dining table, the family shared all that had happened since Uncle Pete's last visit three months earlier. Uncle Pete held out his plate for a second piece of cherry pie and leaned back in his chair.

"Helen, I haven't eaten so well since the last time I was

here," he boomed.

The twins had been reasonably quiet during supper while the adults visited. Now they moved restlessly in their chairs. Jenny, who never hesitated to ask questions, burst out, "Do you have any new stories, Uncle Pete?"

"Yeah, where did you go this trip?" Justin added eagerly.

Uncle Pete's eyes twinkled at the impatient pair as he settled more comfortably into his chair. "As a matter of fact, I haven't been anywhere special since my last visit."

His red beard split in a smile at their disappointed look. "But I do have one little story that might interest you. What can you two tell me about the Incas?"

"Weren't they an ancient empire in South America?" Justin responded thoughtfully.

"Yeah, they built lots of stone cities. There was a picture in our history book last year of that secret stone city up in the mountains," Jenny added.

"Very good! You're both right. The city you're talking about, Jenny, is Machu-Pichu in Peru. In fact, a thousand years ago the Inca had one of the most advanced civilizations in the world. They governed from a high plateau in the Andes mountains around Lake Titicaca, the highest navigable lake in the world. Their empire spread over most of Bolivia, Ecuador, and Peru."

Uncle Pete stopped for a bite of cherry pie. Waving his fork, he continued: "The Inca were most famous for their stone cities and roads—all carved out by hand. Even today's technology can't beat their stone work, and a lot of their roads are still being used.

"But the Inca wasn't the first empire in South America. They took over from another great civilization—one that lasted three thousand years. Tiawanaku, the ruins of that civilization, still lies across Lake Titicaca, in the country of Bolivia."

He looked keenly at his nephew and niece. "Can you tell me what finally happened to the Inca?"

"Didn't Pizarro and just a couple of hundred Spanish soldiers defeat them?" asked Justin. "As I remember, they tricked them and captured their king, and the whole nation just gave up. It seems pretty cowardly to give in to two hundred men!"

"Well, that's what your history books may tell you, but it isn't the whole story. The Inca had a very advanced civilization but also a very cruel one. They conquered hundreds of smaller tribes around them and practiced human sacrifice with their enemies. Everyone but the Inca overlords were turned into slaves.

"When the Spanish arrived, these slave tribes rose up to fight beside them, hoping to win freedom from the Inca. So Pizarro didn't only have two hundred soldiers, he also had thousands of Indian rebels fighting with him. And he had cannon and gun powder, something the Inca had never seen."

"So what happened to the Inca after that?" Justin inquired.

"Their descendants are still there and so are the ruins of their empire. Imagine yourselves, kids, in the capital of Bolivia—the cold winds whistling through the stone walls of Tiawanaku . . . reed boats dancing across the waves of Lake Titicaca to ruined palaces of ancient Inca princes . . ."

Mrs. Parker, glancing in amusement at her spellbound children, interrupted, "I take it you are visiting Bolivia soon?"

"You guessed it! Triton Oil has several offices in the country, and I'll be checking out a bit of trouble at the head office in La Paz. I have some friends in the city, the Evanses. They are a young missionary couple who work with the Quechua Indians, Bolivia's biggest ethnic group. The Quechua are direct descendants of the ancient Inca.

"My business in La Paz should only take a few hours, but I have some vacation time built up. I've been writing my friends in La Paz, and they've talked me into staying in Bolivia a couple of weeks for a real vacation."

"Boy, don't I wish I could go!" Justin exclaimed enviously. "I'm going to have a job just like yours someday, Uncle Pete, so I can see the world the way you do."

Jenny sighed. "It sounds so exciting. You'll take lots of pictures, won't you, Uncle Pete, especially of the Inca ruins? I'd love to see what they look like."

Uncle Pete grinned, looking suddenly like Justin when he was planning some mischief. "Well, as a matter of fact . . ." He glanced across the table at his brother, who mirrored his grin.

"Actually, I thought maybe you'd like to take your own pictures."

Jenny and Justin froze in their seats. "Do you mean it?" they burst out in unison.

Uncle Pete looked apologetically at Mrs. Parker. "I hadn't meant to say anything until I had a chance to talk to you, Helen. Ron wrote that you wouldn't be able to take a family vacation this summer—with that big project Boeing is working on. With the kids out of school, I thought maybe they'd like to come along with me."

Mrs. Parker frowned, and Justin held his breath. He knew his mother didn't like surprises—and the two Parker men had a habit of springing surprises on her.

"I talked the idea over with Ron on the way here from the airport. He said he'd leave it up to you. It would be an educational experience for the children, and I'd really enjoy their company . . ."

"You don't know what kind of trouble these two can think

up!" she protested. "Besides, they're too young to be traveling alone."

"They wouldn't be alone! I'd keep a good eye on them," Uncle Pete promised.

"I don't know . . ." Mrs. Parker said, still frowning. "This is a little sudden. I'll have to talk it over with Ron." She made the mistake of looking up into a circle of pleading eyes, and her expression softened.

"Well, I don't suppose anything can happen to them with you along, Pete." Justin slowly let out his breath as his mother continued, "This is quite an opportunity. If you kids will promise to be careful and do everything your uncle tells you . . ."

She never got a chance to finish her sentence because Jenny was out of her chair and dancing around the table. Even Justin was quivering with excitement.

"Thanks, Mom! You won't be sorry!" Justin said. Jenny exuberantly hugged first her mother, then Uncle Pete, and finally her father. Whirling around the room, she chanted, "We're going to Bolivia! We're going to Bolivia!"

"Well, kids," Uncle Pete said in an amused tone, "I take it you're willing to come?" Their shining eyes alone would have been answer enough.

"Okay, Jenny, let's sit down," Uncle Pete commanded. As they watched Uncle Pete pull out a small notebook from his breast pocket, the twins were reminded that their favorite uncle was also a very capable business executive.

"We will be leaving three weeks from Saturday. In that time we'll need to get your passports, contact the nearest Bolivian consulate, and make travel reservations."

He fastened a stern eye on both children. "I'm allowing you only one suitcase apiece. You'll need warm clothing as well as a few lighter outfits. Bolivia lies south of the equator and, if you remember your geography, it's in the middle of winter right now. It isn't as cold as our northern winters, but it can get pretty chilly—especially since the buildings are unheated.

"Now I'm sure you've had all your vaccinations, but you'll need a few extra shots for traveling—yellow fever, typhoid, malaria . . ."

Jenny poked Justin in the ribs and whispered, "Did you hear that? Yuck! I can't stand shots!"

But Justin was listening with only half an ear. He was seeing visions of ancient golden cities; of haughty Indian warriors marching across a vast, brown plateau with bronze-tipped spears glittering under a deep-blue sky; of thousands of half-naked slaves hauling giant blocks of granite, groaning under the cruel whip of their Inca overseer.

I'm not dreaming! he thought to himself in awe. *I'm really going. You, Justin Parker, are actually going to see the land of the mighty Incas!*

Chapter 2

Land of
the Incas

*H*is nose pressed to the round window of the Boeing 747, Justin watched the barren landscape roll away beneath him. They had been traveling since early morning and were now nearing their destination.

Only an occasional hint of green showed in the valleys nestled far below between rugged, dusty peaks. Here and there Justin could pick out a few crude houses, the same mud-brown as the land around them. The peaks of the Andes mountains didn't seem as high as he expected, until he remembered that even the valleys were 10,000 feet or more above sea level.

Above him a light blinked, commanding in Spanish, *"Abroche tu cinturón."* Below it, another light spelled out, "Fasten your seat belt."

As he snapped his seat belt shut, the plane began to shake. His ears popped as the plane started to lose altitude. Jenny, sitting in the seat next to Justin's, slipped her hand into his. Neither had flown before and, though Justin would never admit it to his twin sister, he was glad to see that she looked as nervous as he felt.

As the plane circled, Jenny gasped in delight. "Look, Justin! Isn't it beautiful?"

A snowcapped mountain, stained rose and orange by the late afternoon sun, filled the horizon. Its majestic peak rose high above the smaller peaks that surrounded a vast plateau.

"That's Mount Illimani," Justin informed his sister. "Uncle Pete says it's over twenty-thousand feet high. They actually *ski* up there. Can you believe it? I wonder how they even breathe."

Justin pulled the airline travel guide out of the deep pocket on the back of the seat in front of him and opened it to the page marked "Bolivia." Three columns down each page showed the words in English, German, and Spanish.

His eyes were caught by a picture of a warmly dressed Indian struggling up the side of a snowy mountain, using a thick rod to help guide a herd of heavily loaded llamas. He read the accompanying paragraphs:

"The *altiplano,* or high plateau of the Andes, home of the original Inca empire, ranges from 9,000 to 16,000 feet in elevation. The international airport of La Paz, capital of Bolivia, sits at 13,500 feet above sea level. The low oxygen level at this altitude and the lack of wind resistance requires a runway four miles long for jets to land on.

"The charming colonial capital of La Paz ranges from 8,500 to 13,500 feet in elevation. You may find yourself suffering from shortness of breath during your stay. Walk slowly, carry little, and take it easy during the first few days of your visit."

How can a city be from eight thousand to thirteen thousand feet high? he wondered. *It must go straight uphill!*

At that moment the plane banked for a landing, and Justin discovered just how this was possible. Below, a thin gray line stretched across a flat, tan desert, ending in a group of low, isolated buildings. A control tower on one side identified these as the airport.

Beyond the high, flat plateau, the ground broke away in a sudden drop of several thousand feet. In an immense, jagged bowl, carved out of the mountains themselves, nestled the modern skyscrapers and colonial buildings of La Paz. Mud shacks clung to the steep sides of the chasm. Zigzagging across the face of the cliffs, dusty roads climbed from the city center to the flat plateau above.

As the plane dipped into the valley, Justin clutched his armrests tightly; it seemed to him that they would fly right into the side of the gigantic crater! But the plane lifted at the last moment and circled around, lining up with the runway. Moments later they were taxiing to a stop.

Uncle Pete leaned over the seat behind them. "Put your jackets on, kids. It'll be cold."

The plane stopped half a kilometer from the airport buildings. Straggling behind the other passengers, Jenny and Justin pulled their jackets tighter as the wind of the *altiplano* hit them. They were breathing hard before they covered half the distance. Justin's shoulder bag felt as though it carried rocks, and he wished he'd followed his sister's lead and handed it over to one of the porters who met the plane.

From behind a wire fence, an excited crowd waved at the incoming passengers. Towering over the dark heads around him, a young man with blond hair waved frantically.

"There's Bob Evans, my missionary friend," Uncle Pete told the children, waving back. Moments later, they were shaking Mr. Evans' hand.

"Stay close to me," the young missionary told them. "We'll need to collect your luggage and clear customs."

As Mr. Evans led the Parkers toward the luggage area, Justin paused to watch soldiers in olive-green leisurely pace their rounds, machine guns slung casually across their backs.

Porters were already unloading the baggage, and Justin helped Uncle Pete pick their luggage off the conveyor belt. As Justin swung his own suitcase down, a large, hairy arm reached past him to grab at a duffel bag. Glancing sideways, Justin raised his eyes, then tilted his head far back to stare at the man looming beside him.

The stranger was obviously a foreigner. His massive head was shaved bald except for a wide strip of dark hair that ran from just above his eyebrows to the nape of his neck. Even for his great height, the man was so wide that he might have looked fat were it not for the rock-hard muscles that bulged under the rolled-up sleeves of his jacket. Without looking down, he tossed the duffel bag over his shoulder and moved away.

Mr. Evans helped the Parkers carry their suitcases over to a series of long counters. Here, uniformed officials dug through each piece of luggage. A large German shepherd, its trainer holding tightly to its collar, sniffed at each bag. Uncle Pete lifted their own suitcases onto one of the counters.

Never shy with strangers, Jenny tugged on Mr. Evans' sleeve. "Why are they looking through our bags? And what's that dog doing?"

Smiling down at her, Mr. Evans answered pleasantly, "They're searching for contraband. There are always a few who try smuggling something illegal in or out. The German shepherd is a trained narcotics dog. He can smell out cocaine or marijuana."

The dog, at that moment sniffing at a khaki-green knap-sack at the next table, whined eagerly. Two soldiers closed in behind a bearded foreigner who began protesting in loud German. Justin, observing the scene with curiosity, noticed that the man who had been standing beside him at the luggage checkout was next in line.

As the customs official ripped open the knapsack with a razor-sharp knife, Justin saw the heavy giant look around nervously, then edge past the counter, his duffel bag still over his shoulder. The customs official glanced up and snapped out an order. A short, thin man in a new, poorly fitting suit pulled at the big man's elbow.

"What do you think you're doing? We don't have anything to hide!" Justin heard him hiss in distinctly American English. The big man shrugged his massive shoulders and dropped the duffel bag on the counter.

Justin turned back to open his own suitcase. Their bags were quickly checked, and fifteen minutes later they were climbing into a red, double-cab pickup.

"Actually," Mr. Evans explained as he started the engine, "We don't have too much trouble with customs coming into Bolivia. Now, *leaving* is another story. They'll check every inch of your suitcases, inside and out."

"Why's that?" asked Justin from the back seat.

"Well, there isn't much contraband coming in. Most smuggling is going the other way. That German they picked up was probably on a through flight home from down in the lowlands. Drugs is the major item since Bolivia is a big producer of cocaine, but Indian artifacts and other valuables are also popular contraband."

The pickup was now swinging down the broad, modern

highway that led to the city center. Mr. Evans glanced at Uncle Pete. "You're sure you don't want us to put you up? You know you're welcome. We don't have many bedrooms, but we've got lots of floor space and sleeping bags."

"We'll do fine in a hotel," Uncle Pete answered. "As I mentioned in my letter, I have some business to take care of, and I plan to do some sightseeing with the kids. We'll be in and out a lot. I know you and your wife are busy, and I don't want to disrupt your whole schedule."

"Well, Pete, Peggy is expecting you for super tonight at least. In the meantime, why don't we get you checked into a hotel."

The pickup was moving into the city now, and Mr. Evans swung away from the main avenue. The children stared at tin or straw-roofed shacks huddled tight against stately, white-washed mansions whose red-tiled roofs peeked out at pass-ersby over the shards of broken glass that guarded their high walls.

As Mr. Evans stopped for a red light, a bent, elderly man, thin rags clutched tightly against the brisk wind, hobbled up to the truck. *"Limosna, limosna,"* he whined, holding out a twisted claw of a hand.

Jenny shuddered as Mr. Evans took his foot off the brake. "Who is that man?" she asked. "What does he want?"

"Just a local beggar," Mr. Evans answered as he dropped a coin out the window.

As he drove on, he continued, "Bolivia is a very poor country. There are a few very rich people, most of them the descendants of the Spanish conquerors. But most Bolivians are Indian or part Indian and live very humbly."

With a grin, he added, "Any more questions?"

Justin and Jenny shook their heads and turned their attention to the strange new sights around them. They were driving through the business section now. The narrow streets were choked with people and vehicles, and Mr. Evans slowed the truck to a crawl. Colonial-style buildings lined the streets in a solid wall, broken here and there by a modern skyscraper.

On all sides, wooden stands filled with goods crowded the sidewalks, and walking vendors shouted their wares. Justin counted shoes, matches, radios, watches, plastic tubs, cotton candy, and a horde of other goods before Mr. Evans pulled into a quiet side street.

Mr. Evans turned to Uncle Pete as he pulled up in front of a long, flat-roofed, two-story building. "You mentioned in your letter that you didn't want to stay in a tourist hotel—that you wanted to practice your Spanish." A sign swinging from a second story balcony announced, *"Hotel Las Américas."*

"This isn't as fancy as the Holiday Inn or the Presidential Hotel, but you'll see more of the real Bolivia here. And you shouldn't run into any other tourists. The clerks may know a bit of English—they study it in school here—but I'm afraid you'll have to get by mainly in Spanish."

"We'll be fine," Uncle Pete answered heartily. "I've picked up a bit of Spanish in my travels. We're looking forward to exploring on our own, aren't we, kids?"

Justin and Jenny nodded doubtfully. Their own Spanish consisted of two words: *"hola"* (hello) and *"adios"* (goodbye).

As Mr. Evans and Uncle Pete lifted the suitcases from the back of the truck, a boy darted around the corner of the building. Thin and wiry, the boy had straight, dark hair flopped over alert black eyes. His hand-woven shirt and faded blue jeans were ragged, but he shone with cleanliness. He held his hand out for Uncle Pete's luggage.

"I carry bags, no?" he inquired in strongly accented English. "Only fifty *centavos.*"

Mr. Evans looked closely at the boy and grinned. "Why, it's Pedro! What are you doing here, Pedro?"

"Hola, Don Roberto," the boy replied with a grin. "I did not recognize your new red truck. I am working in this fine hotel now. I make much money when I carry bags for the *'turistas'* and take them around the city. You like me to help your kind visitors?"

Mr. Evans turned to the Parkers. "Pedro's mother helps my wife with the cleaning now and then. He's a good boy, and responsible. You could do worse than to hire him for a guide."

Justin instantly decided that he liked this boy with the cheeky grin and twinkle in his eyes. "Yes, can't he come with us, Uncle Pete? It would be fun to have someone to talk to.

"How did you learn English, anyway?" he asked the boy.

"My mother work for many important *Americanos,*" Pedro boasted. "I listen and learn good *Inglish.*"

"Mrs. Gutierrez, Pedro's mother, was a maid at the American embassy for many years," Mr. Evans added. "Pedro grew up around *gringos.*"

"But how can you have a job already?" Jenny exclaimed. "You're just a little boy. I'll bet you're not even as old as I am!"

Pedro patted his chest with a thin, brown hand. "I have twelve years," he told her proudly. "I am a man already. I have worked many years."

Mr. Evans explained. "Here, many children work as soon as they are old enough to run errands. Children of poor families have to help earn money for food."

"Just like I have a paper route at home," said Justin. "Only

I get to keep the money I earn."

"It's not as bad as it sounds," Mr. Evans continued. "Most children go to school and only work part-time. You're on winter vacation now, aren't you, Pedro?"

"*Sí,* I can work all day for these fine visitors." He looked hopefully at Uncle Pete.

Uncle Pete laughed and handed the boy a suitcase. "All right, you're hired. But I'll expect you here at the hotel first thing every morning."

"I be there," Pedro answered eagerly. "I show you Lake Titicaca and Inca ruins and—"

Mr. Evans held up his hand. "All right, all right. Let's get these bags inside. You can give your guide talk another time."

At the simple wooden desk in the wide, tiled entryway, Mr. Evans requested two rooms, speaking in clear Spanish. Uncle Pete looked puzzled at the clerk's answering flow of words. "I guess we *do* need a guide," he joked.

The clerk took two keys from the row of wooden boxes behind him and walked around the desk, motioning for them to follow. Pedro eagerly grabbed one of the suitcases and bounded up the stairs behind the clerk.

Mr. Evans was frowning. "I'm afraid even this is turning into a tourist hotel. There are two other Americans staying here . . ."

"Don't be concerned," Uncle Pete reassured him. "Someone from home doesn't sound so bad right now!"

Their rooms were on the second floor and opened onto a long balcony that overlooked a large central courtyard. Shrubs in giant clay pots, the only decoration, drooped unhappily in the winter weather. To Justin's disappointment, the rooms could have been from any motel back home.

"How does a plate of spaghetti sound?" Mr. Evans asked

as they deposited the suitcases inside the door of one room.

Justin suddenly realized how long it had been since lunch. He quickly joined his sister in the back seat of the pickup. Mr. Evans waved to Pedro as he started the engine. "We'll see you first thing in the morning."

He leaned out of the window and added, "By the way, my wife has missed you at Bible Club. Why haven't you been coming?"

The dark-haired boy looked scornful. "I am not interested in children's teaching. You tell me of a God who is kind and merciful and soft. That is not the way life is. One must be strong!"

He stepped back from the vehicle. "I do not need your God! My people have own gods. They are strong and power-ful, and have served us many years."

"God loves all men, but He is also a God of power," Mr. Evans insisted. "He made the world and everything in it. Your mother has come to believe this. Won't you believe too?"

"Your teaching is for women," Pedro answered politely but with conviction. "How can a God who forgives His enemies be strong? Enemies are to be destroyed. No, the old gods are stronger. I will work for your friends, Don Roberto, but I do not wish to hear of your God!"

Mr. Evans didn't argue further but moved sadly away from the curb.

An hour later, at the Evans' simple brick home, the two families crowded around the dining table. Mrs. Evans held a ten-month-old baby in her lap. Another one hammered a spoon against his high chair. The twins were the reason she hadn't met them at the airport.

Justin was still thinking over Pedro's words. Turning to Mrs. Evans at the foot of the table, he asked, "What did Pedro mean by the 'old gods'? Doesn't he believe in one God?"

She thought for a moment before answering. "Pedro is a Quechua Indian. He is descended directly from the Incas, who ruled here long ago. When the Spanish conquerors arrived, they brought their priests as well. The Indians were ordered to become Christians or die.

"Most converted, supposedly, but they continued to worship in their old ways, mixing them with the teachings the Spanish brought. The Indians still pour out offerings of wine to Pachamama, or Mother Earth, whom they now also call Mother Mary. Sacrifices of baby llamas or goats are still made to Inti, the sun god, who they believe is also Saint Peter. Witch doctors still hold power in the country villages, and even in the cities."

Scooping up a spoonful of mashed carrot, she continued, "Pedro's father followed the old ways. He died two years ago, and Mrs. Gutierrez accepted Jesus as her Savior last year. But Pedro is set against following Jesus."

"Maybe we could invite him to church with us," Jenny suggested eagerly. "Tomorrow is Sunday. I'd love to see a Bolivian church."

"Good idea," Mr. Evans approved. "We'll be visiting a Quechua church tomorrow, about a three-hour drive from here. I was hoping you'd want to come with us."

The Parkers agreed to join the Evanses the next day, then Uncle Pete announced they had better be getting back to the hotel. "It's been a long day, and someone needs to get to bed!" He grinned at Jenny, who was almost nodding with sleepiness.

The hotel seemed empty when Mr. Evans dropped them off. Even the desk clerk was gone. "I want you two ready for bed right away," Uncle Pete told the children firmly. "I've got some phone calls to make at the pay phone downstairs. I'll be back in a few minutes."

Justin hurried into the sweat suit he used as pajamas. He was brushing his teeth when Jenny banged open the door of the room he shared with Uncle Pete. "I'm not sleepy anymore!" she announced, plopping down on a bed.

"Me either!" Justin agreed. "Let's sit out on the balcony awhile."

Justin was leaning over the balcony railing, showing Jenny which group of brilliant stars overhead was the Southern Cross, when the door of the next room slammed open. The children jumped back in surprise as a tall, very broad man walked out.

"If we don't get that delivery soon, I'm going to get mad," he growled to someone behind him, running a massive hand over his partially shaved head. "I'm beginning to think your friends are putting us on!"

A small, thin man followed at the other's heels, tugging on a dark suit jacket. "Give them time, Skinner!" he answered crisply, in a peculiarly high, thin voice. "You know how hard it is to come up with a load like that!"

Justin turned around as the two men stepped into the circle of light cast by the open door of their room. "Hey!" he exclaimed in a low voice to his sister. "I saw those two guys at the airport!"

The big man suddenly noticed Justin and Jenny. "Great, just what we need. I thought you said this hotel was empty, Short!"

"Be quiet, you idiot!" the smaller man hissed. "They probably speak English. Who cares, anyhow? They're just kids!"

"Kids have parents!"

Justin was tired of being talked about as though he were deaf. He moved toward his room, but Jenny had already stepped into the circle of light. She held out a hand to the smaller man with her usual friendly smile. "Hi! You must be the other Americans the clerk told us about. I'm Jenny Parker."

"Beat it, kid!" snapped the thin man called Short, ignoring her outstretched hand.

"Yeah!" agreed the giant man called Skinner as he leaned down so close that Jenny could smell his putrid breath. His heavy jowls quivered as he scowled at the two children. "We don't like kids, see? And we *really* don't like kids getting in our way. So you two just keep away from us, got it? We don't want to see you again."

The two men turned and marched off into the night. Justin met his sister's gaze in wide-eyed astonishment. What had they done wrong this time?

Chapter 3

A Church and a Witch Doctor

The bang of a drawer slamming shut woke Justin the next morning. It was still dark, and he couldn't quite make out the hands of his watch. Switching on a bedside lamp, he saw that it was only six a.m. As he swung his feet to the cold tile floor, soft snoring from the next bed told him that Uncle Pete was still asleep.

Justin heard a faint rumble of voices and realized the noise that had awakened him had come from the other side of the wall—the room where the two American men were staying. Padding across the floor in bare feet, he quietly opened the door and slipped out onto the balcony.

The stars were fading against the pale sky of early dawn, and his breath hung white in the cold air. Shivering, he started to swing the door shut, but at that instant the door to the next room slammed open.

The big man named Skinner stomped out, followed closely by the smaller man. Remembering their reaction the night before, Justin stepped back into the doorway, but the two men didn't even glance his way as they hurried by, talking in low voices.

"Those diggers want another raise," the big man grumbled, running his hand across his shaved head.

"They're already getting twice the normal wage!" the smaller man answered sharply.

"They're greedy, that's what!" the big man added.

Justin stepped out to stare after them as they started down the stairs. The deep grumble of the giant Skinner drifted back, "You think those kids will give us any trouble, Short?"

"Of course not!" a high, tenor voice snapped back. "They're just tourists."

Justin slipped back into his room. *They must be archeologists,* he decided. He grinned. Neither of that pair looked much like his idea of an archeologist!

Uncle Pete was now up. Justin could hear his off-key whistle coming from the bathroom. Pulling on a heavy turtle-neck and a pair of jeans, Justin hurried next door to his sister's room. He gave a quick ta-tat, ta-tat on the door, a special rap the two had invented years before to let the other know who was knocking.

A moment later, Jenny flung the door open and said crossly, "Isn't it kind of early to be up?"

"It's almost seven o'clock!" Justin answered. "Didn't you hear Mr. Evans say he'd be here to get us at eight?"

He took a closer look at his sister. "Hey, are you feeling okay? You look awful!"

Jenny was pale, and dark circles lined her eyes. She pushed back her tousled curls with one hand and wearily rubbed her forehead.

"I've got a nasty headache, that's all!" she replied. "Nothing a little more sleep wouldn't help!"

"Sorry! You want me to tell Uncle Pete you can't go with us?"

"No, I might as well get up . . ." Jenny rubbed her forehead again and eyed her brother's casual clothes with distaste.

"You aren't wearing those to church, are you?

"Sure! Mr. Evans said not to dress fancy. We might be sitting on the floor!"

Grabbing some clothes, Jenny hurried into the bathroom. She came out a few minutes later, dressed much like her brother and running a comb through wet curls.

"Weren't those men unfriendly last night?" she commented, frowning at herself in a small wall mirror. "I wonder why they're staying here. Mr. Evans says tourists never come here."

"Maybe they're here for the same reason we are," Justin answered dryly.

"Oh, come on! Don't you think there was something funny about them? Maybe they're criminals hiding out or something!"

"Don't be silly!" Justin knew better than to take his sister's vivid imagination seriously. "They're—"

He was interrupted by a knock at the door. Uncle Pete walked in, carrying a folding card table. He was followed by a stout lady carrying a large metal tray. She cried out in horror at the sight of Jenny's colorless face. Rattling off a long sentence in Spanish, she dropped the tray on the bed and hurried off.

"That was our landlady," Uncle Pete informed them as he set up the card table. "She says Jenny is suffering from altitude sickness."

Uncle Pete studied his niece's pale face. "You certainly

don't look well. Our landlady has gone for some local remedy. If that doesn't work, we'll hunt up some aspirin."

Uncle Pete picked up the tray and motioned Justin and Jenny to sit on the nearest bed. He unloaded a plate of what looked like some sort of turnovers.

"They don't eat much breakfast in Bolivia, but the landlady came up with these. They're called *salteñas* and are a popular breakfast dish. That white stuff is goat cheese."

Uncle Pete was asking the blessing on their meal when the landlady busted in, carrying a small teapot. She gestured at Jenny, then at the teapot.

"Te doy coca para la niña," she beamed, pouring out a cup of pale-green liquid and handing it to Jenny. Gesturing toward Uncle Pete and Justin, she filled two more cups. After placing the teapot on the table, she hurried away.

"I think she said, 'coca tea for the little girl,' " Uncle Pete translated, picking up his own cup. Jenny sipped the green tea, grimacing at its bitter taste.

"It tastes awful, but it seems to work," she said cautiously after a moment. "What is it?"

"From what I've read," Uncle Pete answered, "it's a tea made from the leaves of the coca plant."

"You mean the stuff *cocaine* is made from?" Justin asked.

Uncle Pete grinned at his shocked expression. "Justin, you forget that the coca leaf is used in many medicines. The refined powder we call cocaine is removed from the coca leaf and is a deadly narcotic. But the mild tea made by steeping the leaves is considered the best treatment there is for altitude sickness."

He handed Justin his own cup. "Go ahead and drink it, Justin. It also prevents altitude sickness, and we'll be climbing even higher today."

Justin drank the vile-tasting liquid and had to admit that the tight pressure at the back of his head quickly ebbed away. With a renewed appetite, he bit cautiously into a *salteña*. The strange-looking turnover was filled with a very spicy stew of beef, potato, peas, hard-boiled eggs, and raisins. To his surprise, it was delicious—even if not his idea of a breakfast treat.

Rustling the pages of a local newspaper, Uncle Pete asked, "Seen any sign of our fellow Americans?"

"We sure did!" Jenny answered, reaching for a second *salteña*. Now that her headache was gone, she was recovering her normal high spirits. "They weren't very friendly, either!"

"Hmmph," Uncle Pete grunted, more interested in deciphering the Spanish headlines than in his elusive fellow guests.

A sharp knock sounded at the door. Jenny, jumping to answer it, exclaimed with pleasure, "Pedro! You're here early! Just in time to go with us to church."

"Church! You mean *iglesia*?" The dark-haired boy frowned angrily. "I will not go to any *iglesia*! This is a trick of Don Roberto, is it not? To make me hear of his God!"

Uncle Pete stepped forward. "No, Pedro, Mr. Evans has played no trick. We always go to church on Sunday. It is God's holy day when His people come together to worship Him. You're welcome to come with us, but you certainly don't have to if you'd rather not."

Pedro backed out the door. "I do not go to any *evangélica* church. I will come back tomorrow if you need a guide."

Jenny followed Pedro to the door, her gold-brown eyes pleading. "Please come with us, Pedro! We won't have anyone to talk to if you don't come. You could tell us what everyone is saying. Please?"

"Yeah, please come!" Justin added.

Pedro looked from one to the other. "All right, I come this once," he agreed finally. "But no more tricks."

Soon, the red pickup was bumping its way up one of the narrow, dusty roads Justin had seen from the air. He held on tightly as the pickup jolted over deep ruts. There were no guard rails, and Justin caught his breath at sudden drop-offs of several hundred feet.

Unconcerned, Mr. Evans whipped around narrow U-turns and zipped past oncoming traffic with only inches to spare, while carrying on non-stop conversation. He glanced out the back window to where Uncle Pete and Pedro, hair tossed back by the wind, held on tightly.

Cuddling the twin she carried on her lap, Jenny asked, "What is an *evangélica* church? Why is Pedro so angry about coming?"

Mr. Evans glanced at her in his rearview mirror. "Bolivians call any church that isn't the state church *evangélica*. It really means a church where the gospel or *evangélio* of Jesus Christ is preached."

Justin thought about this as he stared out the window. A year ago at Bible camp, both he and Jenny had accepted Jesus Christ to be their Savior. He remembered the happiness he felt that day. *It would be wonderful if Pedro could come to know Jesus as His Savior, too.*

Soon, he forgot about the other boy in his fascination with the scenes flashing past the window. They were up on the *altiplano* now, and the brown, flat plateau stretched away in every direction. Snowy mountain peaks, dominated by Mount

Ilimani, circled the horizon. They bumped through a village where Indian women squatted in front of their one-room homes, spinning thread on wooden spindles.

"Are these people all Quechua?" Jenny asked, watching the women with interest.

Mr. Evans glanced into his rearview mirror. "No, these villages are Aymara. Most of the country people right around La Paz are Aymara. You have to travel a couple of hours out, as we are doing, to reach the Quechua villages."

Confused, Justin asked, "You mean these people aren't descended from the Inca like Pedro is?"

Mr. Evans smiled. "No, the Aymara are descended from the civilization that built the ancient city of Tiawanaku. We'll take you there tomorrow. The Aymara are very proud of having been here even before the Inca."

Justin watched two men kneading a trough full of mud and straw into large, square blocks. Rows of the adobe bricks dried in the sun beside them. Beyond the village, dug-up plots of land, now barren under the winter chill, showed where the villagers worked to earn a meager existence.

Mr. Evans slammed on the brakes as a herd of sheep and llamas—the pack animals of the Andes—wandered across the road. A small shepherd boy, piping a haunting minor tune on a wooden flute, prodded them along with a sharpened stick. Justin took the opportunity to join his uncle and Pedro in the back. He looked curiously at the Indian boy.

"Have you been up here before?" Justin asked. "Can you speak the Quechua language?"

"I speak Quechua and Aymara," Pedro answered proudly. "I am not one of those city boys who boast that they speak only Spanish. They are ashamed of their Indian blood! My grandfather was great man among the Quechua."

Before Justin could ask about Pedro's grandfather the truck started up again, and the whistling of the wind cut off any further conversation until they reached their destination.

Except for a tin roof, the building looked no different than the few other houses scattered nearby. It was much bigger, but built of the same mud bricks.

"Is *this* a church?" Jenny whispered to Justin.

"Of course, can't you see the sign?" Justin whispered back.

A weathered board nailed over the wide wooden door read, *"Iglesia Evangélica Dios Es Amor."*

"What does that mean?" Jenny asked Pedro.

Pedro shrugged uncomfortably. "It is the name of the church—'God is Love.' It is a stupid name!"

"But God *does* love us," Jenny protested.

"The gods I know don't love. They are strong and have great power to destroy their enemies. My grandfather—"

Pedro's words were cut off as Mr. Evans motioned the children to enter the church. The inside was dimly lit by two small windows cut in the thick adobe walls. To Justin and Jenny it seemed much too small to be a church, but the room was packed wall to wall with people.

The Parter twins had never seen the Quechua people up close before and stared around the room in fascination. The Indian women wore hand-embroidered blouses and brightly colored skirts layered on top of each other until the top skirt stood out like a bell. Many of the women carried a dark-faced baby tied to their back in a thick, homespun blanket. Bows of yard decorated their long, dark braids, and intricate silver earrings dangled to their shoulders.

The dark, homespun pants and shirts of the Indian men were covered against the cold by heavy ponchos, which looked to the children like a blanket with a hole cut in the center.

Most curious were their head coverings. Made of leather, they were designed after the helmets of the Spanish *conquistadores*—conquerors—embroidered with strange, colorful designs. Earflaps hung down on each side of the dark, solemn faces.

Pedro tugged Justin's arm. "Do not stare!" he ordered. "It is very rude!"

Jenny and Justin hurriedly lowered their eyes. A young woman in the back row, openly nursing a tiny baby, smiled shyly and scooted over, making room for them on a bench along the side wall. Justin smiled a thank you and sat down, Pedro and Jenny squeezing in on either side of him. The bench was cool beneath them, and Jenny made a face as she held out dirty fingers to Justin.

"It's made of mud!"

Justin rubbed a finger against the seat and grinned. The benches had been built up from the floor out of more mud bricks. No wonder Mr. Evans had suggested jeans.

A young man dressed in Western clothes, but with the high cheek bones and round, dark face of the Quechua, stepped to the front of the room, strumming a battered guitar. A boy followed him, plucking a high, tinny tune on a small instrument. Somewhat like a miniature guitar, it had ten strings and its gray back was covered with short hair.

"What is *that*?" Jenny asked in a whisper, pointing at the strange instrument.

"It is a *charango*," Pedro answered. "The back is made from the shell of an armadillo. Do you know what this animal is?"

When they both nodded, Pedro continued, "Sometimes they are made of wood. My people make beautiful music with them."

Justin had his doubts about that as the whole congregation stood up and began singing a mournful chorus in a minor key. But the dark faces beamed with joy as they clapped their hands vigorously to the unusual melody.

Looking around, Justin noticed the many bare feet and ragged clothing for the first time. *How can they be so happy when they are so poor?* he wondered. Suddenly, the song leader broke into a tune Justin recognized. The words were strange, but he had sung the song often at home in Sunday school.

"I've got a mansion just over the hilltop," he sang along in English. *This is why they were so happy,* he realized! They had little now, but all the joys of heaven were waiting for them someday.

The singing continued for what seemed hours. At last, Mr. Evans stood up and opened his Bible. There was no Sunday school, but Mrs. Evans invited the small children outside for a Bible story. Smiling, she handed Justin one of the twins and Jenny the other.

Mr. Evans' voice rose and fell as he flipped to different pages of his Bible. The baby Justin held whimpered, and Justin bounced him up and down. Jenny didn't seem to be having any problem.

He tried to understand the strange-sounding words, but his attention soon wandered. *It must be interesting*, he decided, looking around at the absorbed faces.

"What are they saying?" Justin questioned Pedro.

Pedro listened for a moment. "He is teaching about Jesus," he whispered back. "He tells how Jesus loves men and came to the world to die. He tells how He has great power to forgive . . ."

Pedro stiffened. "That is enough! You listen yourself. I am not interested." He leaned back against the wall and shut his eyes for the rest of the sermon.

After the long service, a church family invited them over to their one-room home for dinner. The visitors ate on a long table outdoors.

Justin had almost finished his plateful of boiled rice, potatoes, and chicken doused with a spicy hot sauce, when he noticed that their hosts weren't eating. The woman of the house bent over the outdoor fire, stirring the contents of several large iron pots, while the rest of the family stood and watched their visitors.

"Why aren't they eating?" he asked Mr. Evans.

"It's their custom," Mr. Evans answered quietly. "They give the best they have to their guests. They'll eat what is left after we leave."

His appetite gone, Justin pushed back his plate. "I wish I hadn't eaten so much!"

Mr. Evans laughed. "Don't worry. They would be offended if you didn't eat. They want to do what they can for those who bring the news of Jesus to them."

Somewhat humbled, Justin joined Pedro and Jenny in the back of Mr. Evans' truck. Uncle Pete had chosen to ride inside this time.

"I'm glad we came," he told his sister soberly.

"Me too!" Jenny answered. Red was already staining the snows of Mount Ilimani as the truck jolted slowly away from the simple brick house. Jenny began to sing, as she often did on her way home from church. Justin joined in.

"There is power, power, wonderworking power . . ." the two children shouted to the wind as they rolled along. Justin broke off as he noticed Pedro's frown.

"What's the matter? Don't you like our singing?"

"I do not like your song!" Pedro muttered. "You sing that this Jesus is powerful. What power does He have? At Bible club I have heard of how this Jesus loves and is kind to all men. That is weakness, not strength!"

"Jesus can forgive sins," Jenny answered.

"That is nothing. Any priest can do that," Pedro sneered. "My grandfather—"

"What *about* your grandfather?" Justin demanded. "What's so great about him?"

"My grandfather was a *curandero*, a witch doctor. He had true power. He could kill with a curse. My father told me of how he dried up the crops of his enemies. He even healed a man who stepped on a *chullpa*."

"What's a *chullpa*?" the children chorused.

"You do not know what the *chullpa* is?"

Pedro's thin shoulders hunched as he cast a careful look around at the darkening hills. In a voice so low the children had to strain to hear, he said, "When you go out on the hills on a night of full moon, you may see fire of green or red burning on the ground. But if you should come close, there is nothing there but a rise in the ground. It is a *chullpa*."

"It's probably nothing but phosphorescence," Justin said loudly. "You know, stuff that glows in the dark . . ."

"It is not what you say," Pedro answered angrily. "The *chullpa* is a tomb where some great Inca of long ago lies buried with his treasure. If you see a green fire, there is silver. If the fire is red, there is gold."

"Doesn't anyone try to dig up the treasure?" Jenny asked.

"Some tombs in the ruins have been dug up," Pedro admitted reluctantly. "But the fire on the ground is where the

Inca have put a powerful curse on their tomb. To step on such a *chullpa* brings great sickness and even death. None of my people would go near the places of the *chullpa*."

Justin laughed. "That's just superstition!"

Pedro shivered. "Do not laugh! My aunt stepped on a *chullpa* one night many years ago. She has never walked again. She has a great sore on her foot that never heals."

He looked defiantly at their skeptical faces. "It is true! You ask Don Roberto. But my grandfather had power even over the *chullpa*. He could go to the tombs in safety and take away their curse. He served the old gods, and they gave him that power."

Justin and Jenny looked at each other doubtfully. Justin answered defensively, "God is more powerful than any witch doctor! He took the sin out of my heart and gave me eternal life. That's more than your grandfather could do."

"So you tell me," Pedro retorted. "I have seen the power of the old gods with my own eyes, but what have I seen your God do?"

His black eyes flashed scornfully. "You show me the power of your God! Let me see your God defeat the gods of my grandfather. Then I will believe in your Jesus and worship your God!"

Chapter 4

Curse of
the Incas

Over a breakfast of fresh rolls and cheese the next morning, Justin and Jenny told Uncle Pete the whole story of Pedro's grandfather and the *chullpa*.

"Do you think he was telling the truth, Uncle Pete?" asked Jenny. "I mean, a witch doctor for a grandfather? That's weird!"

Justin swallowed a large bite of bread and added, "I always thought that kind of stuff was just in fairy tales or back in Bible days."

Uncle Pete was still trying to decipher the Spanish headlines of the day's local paper. At their questions, he folded his newspaper and fixed his keen gaze on them.

"Kids, I've been in many parts of the world. I've heard *and* seen some strange things—some fake, but others definitely true. Satan has a lot of power, and he can give strange powers to those who serve him."

Leaning back in his chair, he continued. "The ancient Inca worshiped idols and demons, and where Satan was worshiped, his influence may remain in control."

He smiled at their anxious faces. "I find it very interesting, however, that in all my travels I have never heard of a witch doctor or his curses having power over a person who has put his trust in Jesus. Satan is powerful, but God is far *more* powerful. He will protect His children against the power of the enemy. Does that answer your questions, kids?"

Justin and Jenny nodded soberly. Uncle Pete stood up and tossed his paper onto the bed. "Speaking of the Inca," he said with a twinkle in his green eyes, "Bob Evans has arranged a visit to Tiawanaku today."

To their excited exclamations, he added, "He'll be here in half an hour, so let's get this mess cleaned up."

The twins quickly picked up the remainders of breakfast. Justin carried the breakfast tray down to the hotel kitchen, while Jenny straightened beds. Their rooms tidy again, they went outside and leaned over the balcony, watching the empty courtyard below for signs of Pedro and Mr. Evans.

"I wonder if those two Americans checked out. I haven't heard or seen them since that first night," Jenny commented.

"I'm sure they're still around," Justin answered. "They're probably working."

"Working at what?" Jenny asked curiously. She didn't wait for an answer but turned to wave at Pedro, who was coming up the stairs. A horn honked loudly outside.

"That's our ride," Uncle Pete called. "Let's go!"

"Don't forget the camera!" Jenny reminded Justin as she locked the door of her room. When they had found out about their trip to South America, the twins pooled their savings to buy a small camera. Justin locked his own door now, the camera swinging from his neck by a black strap.

"Now you look like a *real* tourist!" Jenny joked. The two

children hurried down the stairs as the horn honked again. Uncle Pete and Pedro had already climbed inside the red truck.

Justin and Jenny crowded into the back seat of the cab beside Pedro. A pile of straw hats lay on the seat. Mr. Evans explained, "The sun's rays are especially strong at this altitude, even in the winter, and can cause a nasty burn in a short time. You'll need a hat any time you're out in the sun for an extended time."

As Mr. Evans threaded his way through the narrow streets, Justin and Jenny tried on several hats until each found one that fit well enough. Uncle Pete had already picked out a hat, and Pedro was wearing his own battered black bowler.

"Won't the girls at school be jealous when I tell them about this!" Jenny was bouncing up and down with excitement. "Real Inca ruins!"

Mr. Evans glanced back. "Well, yes and no. The Inca certainly lived near Tiawanaku for hundreds of years, but they didn't build it. Tiawanaku was built around two thousand years B.C. At one time, Tiawanaku ruled most of South America. The city stretched as far as the eye could see, and many of the walls and buildings were covered with gold and silver."

"Gold and silver!" Jenny squealed. "Is any still there? Maybe we can find some treasure!"

Mr. Evans smiled. "No, the gold is long gone. When the Spanish came, they stripped the gold and silver from everything they could find. They also destroyed many priceless artifacts. Over the years, most of the tombs and ruins have been looted and much of Bolivia's Indian heritage lost."

Pedro spoke up, frowning. "*Sí,* the *gringos* have stolen much of our treasure!"

"Bolivians have done quite a bit of looting too, Pedro," Mr. Evans answered dryly. "However, there is probably a bit of Inca treasure still buried here and there, maybe even around Tiawanaku. Until recently, the Bolivian government hasn't even allowed archeologists to excavate the ruins. Some excavations have been opened in recent years, but most Bolivians leave the ruins alone, believing the ancient burial grounds are cursed."

Pedro nodded triumphantly at Justin and Jenny. Jenny wrinkled her nose at him as she asked, "Do you think we might find something today?"

"I'm afraid you'd have to turn over anything you found, Jenny. By law, all Indian artifacts belong to the Bolivian government."

"Didn't you say a lot of finds are still smuggled out?" Uncle Pete asked.

"That's right! A poor Indian who digs up a piece of pottery or gold in his field often can't see why he should turn it over to the government when some tourist will pay what to him is a fortune for it. But it's the big-time smugglers, generally Americans or Europeans, who make fortunes selling Indian artifacts to foreign collectors."

They were now up on the *altiplano*. The road was a narrow, dusty ribbon dividing the flat wasteland. A solitary juniper tree and the scattered sagebrush-like plants that covered the *altiplano* provided the only touches of dusty green. Justin and Jenny clung to their seats as the pickup jolted over deep ruts.

After an hour of steady driving, Mr. Evans pulled off into an open field beside the road, an area that had been cleared to serve as a parking lot. A small whitewashed building stood at the edge of the road. There was just one other vehicle there—a long, black touring car.

"No wonder this place is almost empty," Jenny muttered

to Justin. "You practically need four-wheel drive to get out here!"

"This is where we'll buy our tickets," Mr. Evans announced, pointing at the small concrete building. Uncle Pete insisted on buying the tickets, and a smiling, dark-eyed young lady handed over five pieces of white paper stamped, *"Entrada—Cinco Pesos."*

"You kids stay with Pedro now," Uncle Pete ordered. "Don't get out of sight of the main buildings."

Jenny ran eagerly across the road. Justin and Pedro followed more slowly. A wire fence divided the ruins from the road, and the children handed their tickets to the unarmed guard who stood at the wide gate. There were no other guards, and the wire fence looked easy enough to climb over, in spite of several strands of barbwire at the top.

"No wonder there's smugglers," Justin pointed out to Jenny. "You could steal anything you want in there!"

Pedro led the way across the sparse, dry grass. Justin stopped in surprise as what looked like a giant stone swimming pool opened up at his feet.

"Come on!" Pedro called, waving to them from the top of a set of stairs. The three clambered down the stone steps. They were ten feet below the ground here and could see nothing but aging stone around them and a cloudless blue sky stretching overhead.

"Wow, what is this place?" Justin exclaimed, walking over to inspect a massive squat figure that stood in the center of the immense, below-ground-level courtyard. A solemn granite face stared straight ahead, ignoring the humans at its feet as it had for centuries.

"This is the *templo semisubteraneo*," Pedro answered in his best guide's voice. "That means the 'semi-underground temple.' Those are called monoliths." He gestured at the various-sized granite figures that dotted the temple floor. "There once were many more, but some have been taken away."

Jenny reached out and stroked the smooth, cool stone of the wall. She jumped backward with a shriek as a dark face leered at her, wicked eyes twinkling with mischief. Justin was at her side in an instant.

"What's wrong?"

Jenny laughed shakily. "Nothing. I just thought that it was alive!"

Justin saw that what had startled her was a stone head, carved from rock. The wicked twinkle dissolved into sunlight glinting on flecks of metal in the granite eyes. More of the carved heads stretched around the walls in every direction, each with a different face and style of carving. Justin lifted the camera to his eye and carefully snapped several shots of the carvings.

"These are the 'Framed Heads,' " Pedro explained. "Each head and monolith stands for a nation the Tiwanaku defeated in war. They were great warriors. They cut off the heads of their enemies and hung them from their belts to show their bravery."

"They don't sound like the kind of people I'd want for a best friend," Jenny muttered. "Let's get out of here. Those heads give me the creeps!"

"We will go," Pedro announced. "But first you must look here." He guided them to a spot at the far side of the temple.

"Now look up," he commanded. This time it was Justin who stepped back in surprise. A large, square doorway opened up above them. Silhouetted in the doorway was a giant figure that appeared to be floating in the blue sky.

"Wow," exclaimed Justin when he could speak. "How did they get it up there?"

Pedro looked very pleased with himself. "It is not really up in the air at all," he explained smugly. "I will show you."

He led the way out of the subterranean temple. Ahead of them, another set of stairs climbed to the crumbling walls of another temple—this one above ground. A towering block of whole granite stood on each side of the entryway with a third giant block laid across the other two to form a door. Justin and Jenny recognized this as the doorway they had seen floating in the air.

"But where's the statue?" Jenny looked around, puzzled.

"You cannot see it from here," Pedro informed them. "It is on the other side of the Temple of Kalasasaya. Only from below may you see the Mother of All standing in the Doorway of Life."

"Mother of All! Doorway of Life!" Jenny muttered. "That's crazy!"

"How did they get those blocks out here without trucks?" Justin interrupted as Pedro's dark face clouded over. "Each one must weigh tons!"

"Ten tons each," Pedro answered proudly. "No one has ever discovered the secrets of the Tiawanaku. Some of the stones in this temple weigh more than 160 tons. Here, the great gods of the Tiawanaku were worshiped."

"I don't see how they got that big rock up there!" Jenny declared, staring up at the carefully balanced slab that formed the top of the doorway.

"It's just a matter of leverage and . . ." Justin stooped to pick up a small, light-colored piece of rock. It made a faint white line when he rubbed it against the stone step.

"Here, I'll show you how they did it." Justin, who planned to be an engineer someday, made a few quick marks on the step.

But Jenny had turned away. One hand shielding her eyes, she asked, "Hey, aren't those the two Americans staying at our hotel?"

Disgusted, Justin stood up, shoving the small stone into his jacket pocket. Following the direction of her gaze, he instantly recognized the two men—one short and thin, the other tall and broad—who walked rapidly toward the temple. At the sound of Jenny's voice they stopped. The short man pointed and said something to his companion in an angry voice.

"Now, don't you think that's odd?" Jenny demanded. "Why are they so determined to avoid us?"

"Oh, who cares!" Justin answered in an annoyed voice. "They're archeologists. They're probably here working!"

"How do you know that?" Jenny demanded. Justin repeated the conversation he had overheard the day before.

"Well, it wouldn't hurt them to be a little more friendly!" Jenny insisted stubbornly.

Jenny turned to follow Pedro into the Temple Kalasasaya, but Justin paused to shoot one last photo of the ruins spread out behind him. He had forgotten the two Americans, but as he focused, they moved into view. He could see their faces clearly as he shot the picture.

It was the last shot on the roll, and he was rewinding the film when he heard an angry shout from below. He looked down to see the big man named Skinner running up the steps toward him.

"Give me that camera!" he growled roughly and grabbed it from Justin's hand. Opening the back, he yanked out the film.

"Give that back!" Justin yelled, snatching the camera back. In answer, the big man shoved the roll of film into his pocket.

"Hey, you can't do that!" Justin protested angrily. "I'm going to call the guard!"

The smaller man named Short was instantly at their side. "What are you doing, Skinner?" he demanded sharply in his high, thin voice. "We don't want any trouble here!"

The big man subsided and stepped back, scowling, but he didn't return the film. Turning to Justin, Short said soothingly, "I'm sorry about this. My friend here has this thing about having his picture taken."

He shoved a five dollar bill into Justin's hand. "Here! This should cover the damage." With a sharp order to his large friend, he turned and walked quickly down the stairs.

Justin burned with anger as he stared after the two men. It wasn't so much the film. He had spare rolls, and the five dollars more than covered the cost of the lost film. But there were irreplaceable pictures on that roll!

What a fuss over one picture! he fumed. He considered calling for Uncle Pete or the guard, but the two men were already out of sight. He turned to join Pedro and Jenny inside the temple.

Inside, Justin saw another vast courtyard dotted with granite statues. In a straight line with the entrance stood the monolith they had seen from below ground. Using exact mathematics, the city's builders had placed the thirty-foot-high monolith in a direct line with both gates so as to be seen from the underground temple and from no other angle.

"This is *Pacha Mama*," Pedro was telling Jenny. "The name means 'Mother Earth'—she who gives life." Jenny and Justin stared up at the massive figure who held some sort of cup in each hand.

A long stone wall divided the area to Justin's left. He was fascinated with the elaborate stonework, and he pushed his anger to the back of his mind as he studied the stones.

"They fit together so perfectly!" he exclaimed. "Just imagine cutting that many huge stone, without any machines!" Pedro shrugged his thin shoulders and looked bored. None of this was new or exciting to him.

Justin shut his eyes, ignoring the grass creeping through cracks and the weathered walls. In his mind he saw the great city full of life—the golden buildings on fire with the blaze of the sun; warriors pushing through the crowd, their grisly trophies of war hanging from leather belts; an Indian noble in a litter staring haughtily at the common people, his gold chestpiece and armbands glittering with emeralds and turquoise.

How exciting it would have been to live back then! Justin thought. Then he remembered the bloody battles and human sacrifice and decided the time he was living in now really wasn't so bad.

As he turned to look at the *Pacha Mama* a low, spooky voice inquired, "Justin, are you going to nap all day?" Startled, he whirled around, but neither Jenny nor Pedro was in sight. A moment later Jenny peered around one end of the low stone wall.

"Over here," she called, looking pleased with herself. When Justin joined her, she showed him a hollowed-out cone in the stone wall. When Justin whistled into the opening, his voice reverberated across the courtyard.

"Wow!" he exclaimed. "Their own loudspeaker system!"

Pedro nodded. "Yes, the priests spoke to the people from here. They thought it was the voice of a god."

They were leaving the temple area when a man in Indian homespun clothing crept up to Justin. He looked much like the villagers Justin had seen the day before. "*Tesoro!* Treasure!" he whispered. Before Justin could move away, he swung open his ragged coat and showed Justin a small stone figure that looked like the much smaller twin of the *Pacha Mama* monolith at the back of the courtyard. The six-inch figure was encrusted with earth and looked as ancient as the hills.

"Only forty pesos!" the man whispered, glancing around furtively. "A great treasure!"

Jenny, too, had pressed close to look at the miniature monolith when Pedro suddenly pushed his way in. He spoke a few sharp words to the Aymara villager, and the man walked away reluctantly.

"It is not worth a peso!" Pedro explained with a grin. "The villagers carve the *Pacha Mamas* from stone, then bury them a few weeks. The tourists pay well for the 'great treasure.' "

"But that's cheating!" Jenny cried hotly. "We should report it to the guard!"

Pedro shrugged. "The tourists know it is illegal to buy artifacts. It is only their fault if they are cheated."

They were now at the temple entrance. Skipping down the steps, Jenny suddenly called out, "Look! There are those guys again!"

Justin's eyes followed Jenny's pointed finger. The two Americans had rounded the corner of the temple and were walking rapidly toward the children.

Justin scowled. "Let's get out of here. I don't want anything more to do with them!"

"I don't think they can see us here anyway," she answered. "See? They're going toward that hill."

Sure enough, the men had walked by without glancing their way. Beyond the ruins was a hill perhaps a hundred feet high and several hundred feet long. Its sides and flat top were too even to be natural.

"I think it is time to go," Pedro said loudly. "Your uncle will be looking for you." Jenny and Justin stared at him in surprise.

"I'm not ready to go," Jenny answered sharply. "Isn't that a cave or something up there? It looks interesting. Let's go see." She started in the direction of the two men.

"No, do not go!" Pedro called, running after her. Justin followed on his heels. Pedro caught Jenny by the arm and pulled her to a stop. The mound was only fifty yards away now; the opening Jenny had seen was a third of the way up the steep hillside. They could now see that a brick wall had been built a short way into the cave, blocking the opening. Large boulders were piled up against the bricks.

"I guess we can't get in!" Jenny grumbled with disappointment.

"You do not want to go there!" Pedro answered urgently. "It is a very bad place!"

The two Americans, only a few yards ahead, halted at the sight of the trio. "It's those pesky kids again," the shorter man grunted.

Jenny pulled away from Pedro. "What's the matter? Why shouldn't I go there, Pedro? Look! A piece of the wall has crumbled away . . . I'll bet we could get in."

Catching sight of Justin, the massive Skinner scowled and edged away, but the shorter man stopped, obviously eavesdropping on the children's discussion.

Pedro looked around nervously and lowered his voice. "It is the *Cueva de la Inca Rey*—the Tomb of the Inca King. They say a great Inca king was buried there long ago. He put a very powerful curse of death on the man who disturbs his resting place. They say there are tunnels leading deep into the ground and much treasure, but no one will go near to search for it."

Justin groaned. "Oh, come on, Pedro! Not another horror story!"

"It is true!" Pedro insisted. "Everyone knows that it is a very bad place. In past time men tried to steal the treasure, but none who entered the *cueva* ever came out again. You see that brick wall? So many were lost to the curse that our government sealed the door. Now no one may disturb the burial place again."

At his words, the big American turned back and gave an ugly laugh. "Hey, kid," he growled, grabbing Pedro by the shoulders. "Are you saying there's treasure in there, and you people are letting it rot because of some stupid superstition?"

Pedro stood his ground unafraid, meeting Skinner's eyes squarely. "Once, before the cave was sealed, another American came to Tiawanaku," he answered scornfully.

"Oh, yeah?" Skinner growled. "So what happened?"

"He too laughed at the curse of the *cueva*," Pedro continued. "He said there must be some strange gas inside that killed people. He put on a suit with air like an astronaut and said he would bring out the treasure of the Inca. He went inside the cave."

The big man thrust his heavy, ugly face close to Pedro's. "Well, kid, tell us! Did he get out with anything?"

"He was lost for several days, but at last he made his way out of the *cueva*," Pedro answered soberly.

His audience waited expectantly. His black eyes bright with triumph, Pedro broke into a malicious grin at the sudden greed on the two Americans' faces.

"No, he had no treasure with him. When his friends found him, he knew nothing of what he had done or where he had been. He was *loco*. He had become what you *gringos* call completely insane!"

Chapter 5

An Overheard Plot

The short, thin American tugged on his companion's sleeve. "Let's get out of here, Skinner!" he commanded in his curiously high voice. "This kid's giving me the creeps."

Skinner laughed uneasily as he backed away from Pedro. "Okay, Short. We've wasted enough time already. These natives always have a few stories like that for the tourists. You can't believe a word they say!"

The two turned and marched off along the base of the mound. Pedro stared after them angrily. Justin turned to his sister.

"I agree with them; let's get out of here. I don't think Uncle Pete would want us exploring out here."

Jenny shrugged and started walking back toward the main temple complex. "Okay. I just lost my appetite for exploring anyway." She grimaced. "You couldn't pay me to go near that place again!"

Justin glanced back at the *Cueva de la Inca*. The blocked opening dark against the hillside, it now seemed menacing and eerie. Unaccountable goose bumps rose on Justin's arms. He hurried after the others, thrusting the strange mound out of his mind.

The trio found Uncle Pete and Mr. Evans in the *Templo Semisubteraneo*, inspecting the row of carved heads. The sun shone brightly directly overhead, and the twins were grateful for the shade the straw hats provided. By now, two tourist buses had arrived on the scene. Cameras clicked and voices exclaimed in a dozen different languages.

Uncle Pete glanced at his watch. "Twelve o'clock on the dot!" he boomed. "Let's see about scraping up some lunch."

Mrs. Evans had packed them a picnic lunch of sandwiches and fresh fruit, but Jenny and Justin were attracted to the appetizing odors coming from the little wooden food stands that lined the road outside the barbwire fence. A withered old lady, in a handwoven shawl, fanned the coals under a homemade barbecue. Chunks of meat, potato, and onion threaded on long, hand-whittled sticks sizzled deliciously over the flame.

She turned the shish-kebobs to brown the other side, and Justin and Jenny watched in fascination as her long braids bobbed inches from the glowing coals. Jenny sighed in relief when the old lady sat back without catching on fire.

Next to her, an Indian woman shyly offered a basket of tamales wrapped in corn husks. An old-fashioned ice cream cart bounced by. It had been converted into a grill for hamburgers and plump highland sausages.

"Please, can't we try something here?" Justin and Jenny begged Uncle Pete. "We can get sandwiches back home."

"Well, go ahead," Uncle Pete agreed finally. "But don't blame me if you come down with a case of dysentery."

By pointing and using their few words of Spanish, the twins managed to pick out a pair of shish-kebobs. Jenny chose a juicy sausage wrapped in a bun, and Justin decided to try the hamburgers. From a soda vender, they also picked out a bottle of soda pop for each person in the party.

Justin carefully counted out the Bolivian pesos Uncle Pete had given him, then settled down on the grass with his booty. Pedro grinned as Justin bit into his hamburger and choked.

"It's hot!" he exclaimed, grabbing at his bottle of cola. "What's in it?" Lifting up the corner of the thick, heavy bun, he discovered that Bolivian hamburgers included a fried egg, french fries, and a liberal amount of hot sauce. He tried a smaller bite and decided it was really quite good.

Lunch over, Uncle Pete looked at his watch again. "Well, are you kids ready to head back? I'm sure Bob—Mr. Evans, that is—has things to do."

"Oh, don't worry about me," Mr. Evans said, hurriedly swallowing the last of his egg sandwich. "I've got all afternoon."

"Oh, please, can't we stay a bit longer, Uncle Pete?" pleaded Jenny. "We'll never get another chance to come here . . ."

Justin suddenly remembered his lost roll of film. "Yeah, and I've got to take more pictures!" he muttered glumly.

Uncle Pete stretched out on the grass, his arms behind his head. "I don't know where you kids get your energy. Okay, you've got two hours. Be at the car by three o'clock. I'm going to take a bit of a nap." He waved them off, then tilted his hat against the sun.

The three children spent the next half-hour wandering through the main buildings again, Justin quickly filling up another roll of film. Jenny perched on the edge of a low stone wall, gazing restlessly around the ruins.

"I want to see something new!" she complained. "We've

already been through all this. What's across the road there? Look at all those broken-down walls in the field. And those houses over there are so cute. Let's explore."

"There is nothing to see," Pedro answered sharply. "It is a village like any other village. And those ruins in the field have not been excavated yet."

"Well, I want to see what's over there. Are you coming, Justin?"

"I guess so. You're coming too, aren't you, Pedro?"

Pedro sat down and leaned against the outer wall of the Temple Kalasasaya. "If you wish to go, go! There is nothing to see, and it is too hot to walk more. I will stay and have a siesta."

He slid further down, folding his arms behind his head. Justin and Jenny left him stretched full length on the ground, his black bowler tilted to cover his face. Stepping over a strand of barbwire, they hurried toward the field they had glimpsed.

Broken granite boulders were scattered throughout the sparse grass. Some were massive, but most protruded only a few inches out of the ground. Hordes of black grasshoppers scattered in all directions with every step the twins took.

Justin kicked against something solid in the grass. Bending down, he tugged at an object half-buried in the packed earth. Pulling it free, he found that he was holding a broken shard of pottery. It was caked with dirt, but when Justin knocked the piece against a stone wall, he discovered faint red and black markings under the earth.

"You know we aren't supposed to take stuff!" Jenny reminded him as he thrust the piece of pottery into his jacket pocket. His fingers felt the small stone he had put there earlier, and he pulled it out.

"I know!" he answered, absently shoving the stone back

into his pocket. "I'll give it to the man at the gate. Who knows, maybe he'll say we can keep it. It can't be worth a whole lot!"

They walked around the field again. "Pedro was right," Justin declared. "There's nothing to see here!"

"Let's explore the village," Jenny suggested. "After all, they're real live Incas."

Beyond the unexcavated ruins, the ground dipped to form a shallow valley. A cluster of adobe homes huddled on the banks of a narrow creek. The sandy flats sloping up from the nearly dried-up stream bed showed it would widen into a respectable river with the arrival of the annual rains.

Outside the nearest hut, three small, ragged children danced in a circle, holding hands and playing the Quechua equivalent of "Ring Around the Rosies." As Justin and Jenny walked by, they stopped their game, staring at the two strangers with solemn, dark eyes. Jenny smiled at them, and Justin called, "Hello!" Startled, the children scurried into the hut.

Behind the hut, the twins watched the woman of the home lift small, flat loaves of bread out of an igloo-shaped clay oven with a giant-size wooden spatula. She, too, just stared in reponse to their smiles and hurried away around the side of the hut.

Down at the stream edge, other women beat clothes against flat, well-worn boulders. Jenny was interested to see girls half her age scrubbing vigorously beside their mothers. Clean clothes, spread over low, thorny bushes along the banks, bleached white in the brilliant sun.

From down in the shallow valley, the two could not see the ruins of Tiawanaku. The sun had moved well to their right before Justin remembered to check his watch.

"Oh, no—it's twenty to three already! We'd better get

back now, Jenny. Uncle Pete's not going to be very happy if we're late."

They were far down the river bed now and quickly clambered up the slope of the shallow valley. When they stood once more on the high plateau, they gazed around in dismay. The ancient city of Tiawanaku was nowhere in sight. Low, rolling hills spread out in front of them.

"Come on!" Justin commanded, setting off toward the nearest rise. "It must be just over that hill there."

"Don't you think we should go back the way we came?" Jenny asked.

"We'd never get back in time that way!" Justin answered. "You know how Uncle Pete is about being late!"

Justin led the way up one low knoll, then down the other side. He continued confidently up the next rise, but when he reached the top, he saw nothing ahead but more rolling hills. Even the stream was now out of sight. He continued on for a few moments more, then stopped, looking around for something familiar.

"What's the matter?" Jenny demanded impatiently. "You didn't get us lost, did you?"

"Give a guy time to think!" Justin snapped. Then he admitted reluctantly, "Well, I'm not too sure which way we should be going. All these hills look alike!"

"No problem," Jenny said, her brown eyes glowing with a sudden idea. "We'll ask directions at that house over there." She waved toward a metallic sparkle to their left, just visible over the next rise. A closer look showed the glimmer to be a peaked tin roof.

"Sure," answered Justin scornfully. "And how do you plan to ask? With sign language?" He hated asking directions or admitting he was lost.

"Exactly! Just wait and see! Come on, or we'll be late."

Jenny began running toward the lonely house, and Justin trotted behind reluctantly. They stopped at the edge of the grassless yard. One lone tree, its wide branches giving evidence of water close by, swayed gently in the slight breeze, providing welcome shade to the baked earth.

This family must be well-off, for Bolivians, Justin thought, noticing a Honda motorcycle standing against one adobe wall—not to mention the tin roof in place of the usual thatch. A shiny new shovel leaned against the front door. Latin-style country western music blasted from the one small window.

"Hello," Jenny called. The only answer was a menacing growl. Around the corner of the house rushed a scrawny black mongrel. Every rib stood out with the effort of his wild barking. It paused when it saw the two strangers.

"Nice doggy, nice doggy," Jenny called out nervously, holding out a hand to make friends. The dog's response was to bare his yellowed fangs again in an ugly snarl. It moved forward slowly, growling continuously, and the twins backed up until they reached the shade of the big tree. Justin leaned down to pick up a dry branch beside the tree trunk. The dog lunged forward, barking wildly.

"Get up in the tree, Jenny," Justin told his sister in a low voice. He struck threateningly at the dog, who backed up a few feet. Jenny, pale with fear, climbed for the nearest branch that would hold her. Dropping his stick, Justin scrambled up behind her. No sooner had his feet cleared the ground than the black mongrel lunged. Jaws snapping viciously, it threw itself high into the air, its fangs brushing the bottoms of Justin's sneakers.

"*Véte!*" A stone was hurled through the air, striking the black dog in the ribs. The dog dropped to its belly, whining.

There was a loud snap of fingers, and the dog slunk around the side of the hut.

Still clinging to the branch, Justin and Jenny gave a joint sigh of relief and looked around for their rescuer. A tall man in Western clothes leaned against the doorjamb of the hut. A bowler hat crushed his dark, kinky curls, and he carried what the twins recognized as an expensive radio/double-cassette player, which still blasted out music. As he stepped into the sunlight, he slipped on a pair of sunglasses.

Jenny giggled. "Does he think he's a movie star?"

Waving his hands expressively, the man poured out a flow of smooth Spanish; Jenny and Justin didn't understand a word. The children slid down the tree trunk as the man walked over to meet them.

Wiping a dirty hand against dusty jeans, Jenny held it out in greeting. "Thank you for saving us!" she said. Assuming from his blank expression that he didn't understand, she waved her arm toward the hills and asked hopefully, "Tiawanaku? Please!"

In the shade of the big tree, the stranger took off his sunglasses. His dark-brown eyes crinkled with amusement. "You wish to go to Tiawanaku?" he asked politely.

"Oh, you know English! Great!" Jenny exclaimed. "Yes, we're lost. We have to get back right away."

"My name is Pepe. I study one year in U.S.A.," the curly-haired man told them proudly. "My English is pretty good, no? I help you get home."

Justin interrupted, "Uh, sir, is that your dog? I mean, could you keep hold of him till we get away?"

A wide grin split the tanned face. "You might say he go with house. You need not be afraid. You must go in that direc—"

As he raised his arm to point, he suddenly froze, his smiling expression slowly changing to shocked fear. Recovering himself, he grabbed the surprised twins by the arm and pushed them toward the corner of the building.

"Go! *Véte! Fuera de aquí,*" he shouted, lapsing into Spanish. Jenny held back. "But . . . the directions."

The man didn't answer. His face was set with anger and fear. He whistled loudly. Justin grabbed Jenny's arm and broke into a run as a loud yapping broke out behind them. Glancing back as they ran, he saw the black mongrel loping along after them.

The dog followed them for a few hundred yards. Then, with one last growl, he turned back to his guard duties. Justin and Jenny ran until they collapsed onto the grass behind a patch of bushy, sagebrush-like *tola,* clutching their aching sides. Justin was sure they were out of sight here, but he raised his head cautiously so that only his eyes showed above the scratchy bushes that shielded them.

"So that's what they are!" he exclaimed. "Boy, am I ever stupid!"

"What *who* are?" Jenny gasped, still out of breath.

"I'll show you!" Justin answered grimly. "Look!" Jenny inched up beside him, staring back the way they had come. Entering the barren yard they had just left were two figures she recognized—one tall and broad, the other short and wiry. They both carried knapsacks over their shoulders.

Walking right behind them, two Aymara men carried an assortment of shovels and pickaxes. The strange man named Pepe, black dog at his side, hurried to meet the two Americans, his hands in the air as he talked energetically. Justin strained to hear his words, but he was out of earshot.

"That's funny!" Jenny exclaimed. "What are they doing

here? And why did that man shove us out of there? We weren't hurting anything!"

"I've got a good idea," Justin told her gloomily. "Remember how you thought those guys might be criminals? Well, I'm beginning to think you were right. That man was afraid of those two. He was afraid of them finding us there."

"But you said they were archeologists!" Jenny protested. "See? They're carrying digging tools."

"Archeologists aren't the only ones who dig. I'll bet those guys are smugglers, digging up Inca artifacts like Mr. Evans told us. No wonder that Skinner didn't want his picture taken!"

"What picture?" Jenny asked curiously.

Justin explained quickly. Jenny still looked puzzled. "But none of us would have recognized his picture anyway! And no one else would ever have seen it!"

Justin grinned. "Maybe he didn't think of that. I get the impression he isn't very smart!

"Look!" Jenny pointed. "They're leaving again!"

Sure enough, the two Americans were walking away from the house now. The three Bolivians followed behind, carrying their tools, the black dog still at Pepe's side.

"Come on!" Justin commanded urgently, jumping to his feet. "We've got to see what they're up to!"

"We can't follow them! We're already late!" Jenny protested. "You know how mad they got when they saw us before. And Uncle Pete's going to be mad too if we don't get back soon. We weren't supposed to come this far."

"He'll understand when we tell him what happened," Justin assured her a little doubtfully. "If these guys are up to something, it's our responsibility to find out and tell the police. Besides, maybe they'll lead us back to the ruins. Now, are you coming, or am I going alone?"

"Oh, I guess!" Jenny agreed reluctantly, standing up slowly and brushing bits of debris from her clothes.

"Hurry up!" Justin urged impatiently. "They're getting away!"

By now, the five men had disappeared around a bend in the terrain beyond the tin-roofed house. Justin trotted in the direction they had gone, Jenny close behind. By the time they were out of breath again, they could hear muffled voices.

Justin pulled his sister to a halt and pointed. Not far ahead, the five men still walked rapidly without looking back. Keeping out of sight but still within earshot, the two children now followed more slowly.

They were climbing a low ridge the men had just disappeared behind when Justin realized the muffled voices had grown louder. He placed a finger to his lips, motioning to the side of the ridge. Jenny nodded that she understood, and they both crept up the ridge as quietly as they could, slipping occasionally on the loose shale.

They had reached the end of the uneven land that ran along the river bed. The top of the ridge gave a clear view of the plateau stretching off to their left. The twins were relieved to see the ruined temples of Tiawanaku only a half mile away. Voices rang out clearly from the other side of the ridge.

Lying flat on his stomach, Justin inched toward the voices. Taking cover behind a small boulder that perched on the very edge of the ridge, he lay quietly, watching the scene below. He felt Jenny inch up beside him, and she too froze.

In a shallow gully below them lay a mound perhaps ten feet high and a hundred feet long. Like the *Cueva de la Inca*, its side were too regular to be a natural hill. The two Aymara men were already digging deep into the baked ground while Short and their curly-haired friend sifted through a pile of loose soil. It was evident from the turned-up piles of earth that the excavation had been going on for some time.

Skinner was pulling a strange-looking object from his knapsack. Justin recognized the object immediately. The summer before, his father had taken him gold prospecting in the Montana Rockies. "A metal detector," he muttered.

"Maybe they really are archeologists," Jenny whispered in Justin's ear.

"They wouldn't be so sneaky if they had permission to dig," Justin whispered back.

As the children watched intently, Skinner began running the metal detector over the surface of the mound. "Haven't found anything yet!" he called loudly after a few minutes. "Maybe there's nothing here. We shouldn't have listened to those villagers' wild tales."

"Just keep moving!" Short snapped back. "This spot isn't that important anyway. We've got that Island of the Sun delivery coming in tomorrow. If Pepe here comes through on that, we'll have a pretty good haul this trip."

"Yeah, if he comes through! I wouldn't trust him too far."

Justin put his mouth to Jenny's ear. "We'd better get out of here. Uncle Pete will know what to do about these guys. Let's go!"

Still flat on his stomach, he crawled back from the edge until he could sit up without being seen from below. He touched Jenny's ankle and motioned for her to follow. Jenny rose to her hands and knees, but as she started her backward crawl, her hand knocked away a fist-sized rock. She grabbed for it, but the rock rolled toward the edge, gaining speed.

Before she could move, the rock tumbled over the edge of the ridge, followed by a small avalanche of pebbles. They heard a crash below and an angry shout. Then a gravelly voice bellowed, "Hey! There's someone up there! Get him before he gets away!"

Chapter 6

Gold in the Dark

"**C**ome on! We've got to get out of here! Fast!"

Justin jumped to his feet and grabbed his sister's hand. No longer trying to be quiet, the two children scrambled down the rough slope, slipping and sliding through the loose shale.

They paused momentarily at the bottom. Then Justin, remembering the glimpse of Tiawanaku from the top of the ridge, pointed left, and they ran as fast as their tired legs could carry them along the shallow ravine at the bottom of the ridge. They could now hear the shrill barking of the black dog.

Rounding one last rise, the twins suddenly broke into the open. The ruined walls of Tiawanaku loomed only a few hundred yards away. But the ground between them and the safety of the ruins was flat, offering only a few stunted bushes for cover, and the men behind them would be upon them in seconds.

Justin hesitated, looking around frantically. The baked earth of the high plain absorbed little water, even during the rainy season, and the runoff had carved shallow, winding ditches across the face of the plateau. The limited cover these ditches offered was the twins' only hope of escape.

Already, the mongrel's barking sounded much closer. The two children sprinted toward the nearest ditch. They jumped into it just as the barking dog broke into the open. The narrow crevice was just deep enough to hide them if they lay flat.

Hardly breathing, Justin lay motionless, expecting the dog to be on them any minute. But a sharp voice yelled an order, and the barking stopped.

Jenny moved beside him. "Did they see us?" she whispered breathlessly.

Justin shook his head nervously. "I don't know!"

"Well, I'm not going to lie here and wait for them to catch us!" Jenny answered firmly. She raised her head until her eyes barely showed over the edge of the ditch, her brown curls blending into the dusty background.

"They're there, all right!" she said a moment later, dropping back down. "They're standing on top of the rise, looking this way. But I don't think they saw us."

Justin didn't dare *lift* his head to see. His bright red hair would be a dead giveaway. The two children lay motionless for a full five minutes, then Jenny slowly lifted her head again.

"They're leaving!" she whispered triumphantly. She started to sit up, but Justin pulled her back down.

"Give them time to get out of sight!"

Justin kept an eye on his watch. Not until another five minutes had passed did he motion for Jenny to take another look. She raised her head again, then jumped to her feet.

"They're gone! Let's go!"

Justin too raised his head. The low rise ahead of them was now empty, and he could see no sign of the strange Americans or their helpers. He too jumped to his feet.

"We've got to tell Uncle Pete about this right away," he said, breaking into a run again. Jenny groaned but began running as well, her long legs easily keeping up with her brother.

As they neared the ruins, they saw Pedro standing at the top of the broad temple steps, his hand shading his eyes as he searched the horizon. Catching sight of them, he waved and ran to meet them. Breathless, the twins dropped to the ground and waited for Pedro.

Pedro's dark face was anxious. "Where have you been gone to? Three o'clock has gone long ago. We search for you everywhere! Your uncle is very worried."

He took in their rumpled appearance. "What has happened to you?"

"We're really sorry we're late," Justin apologized. "But just wait till you hear what we've been doing." He quickly filled Pedro in on the adventures of the last couple of hours.

"I'm sure they're stealing Inca artifacts," Justin finished. "Once we tell Uncle Pete, he'll tell the police and have them arrested. That will be the end of their little game!"

Pedro frowned. "I do not think you understand our country. The police will do nothing to these men. They will not believe your story. You have no . . . no *evidencia*—what is the word?"

"Evidence," Jenny supplied.

"Yes, you have no evidence. There is no law that says a man may not dig in a field. The *policía* will not bother *Americanos* for that."

"But we saw the mound!" Jenny protested.

"There are many mounds in the *altiplano*. And they will be gone long before you can tell anyone. No, you will not catch these men."

Justin frowned thoughtfully. "What if they actually caught

them with Inca gold? Would they arrest them then?"

"Oh, yes. Stealing my country's treasures is a great crime. But you would have to be very sure. The police do not like to make trouble with the American embassy."

"Well, I have an idea," Justin said. He stood up, brushing off the tan-colored dust that covered his clothes. "Come on, we'd better go apologize to Uncle Pete and Mr. Evans."

The two men were too relieved over Jenny and Justin's safe return to scold much. The twins explained that they had gotten lost and told in detail of their hair-raising adventure with the black dog. They left out their run-in with the smugglers, though Justin did mention they had seen the other two Americans.

At the gate, Justin remembered the piece of pottery he had found and handed it to the guard. The guard examined the grimy piece carefully, then handed it back with a flourish and a smiling flow of Spanish words.

"He said that it is worth nothing," Pedro translated. "You may keep it as a reminder of our country."

Justin carefully wrapped the ancient fragment of pottery in his handkerchief and thrust it back into his pocket.

As they drove toward La Paz, Justin listened with only half an ear to Jenny's excited chatter and Uncle Pete's deep answers. They were dipping down into the valley when Justin suddenly asked, "Uncle Pete, do you think we could visit the Island of the Sun tomorrow?"

"You mean on Lake Titicaca? Where did you hear of the Island of the Sun, Justin?"

"Oh, I heard somebody mention it," he answered vaguely. He added hopefully, "I'm sure it would be educational. Please, couldn't we go there tomorrow?"

Uncle Pete laughed. "Yes, of course we can. I hadn't

planned on leaving La Paz without visiting Lake Titicaca. Pedro can help me rent a car, and we'll drive up in time to have lunch at the lake."

Once back at the hotel, Justin and Jenny returned their straw hats to the pile on the back seat. Noticing this, Mr. Evans urged, "You'll need those for your trip tomorrow. You might as well keep them as long as you're here in La Paz."

Bent over a map early the next morning, Pedro and Uncle Pete were making plans. "We'll drive to Copacabana for lunch, then rent a boat to tour the lake," Uncle Pete decided at last.

"And the Island of the Sun?" Justin asked anxiously.

"We'll be sure not to miss that," Uncle Pete promised.

Uncle Pete swung the rented car around the curves to the plain above as expertly as Mr. Evans had. Pedro sat beside him, giving directions and pointing out objects of interest to the twins in the back seat. Jenny exclaimed over each new sight, but Justin slumped over, quiet and preoccupied.

"What's the matter?" Jenny asked curiously.

Justin looked up. "I was wondering if those guys will really be on the Island of the Sun today. Wouldn't it be great if we could catch them in the act?"

Pedro had turned around to face them. "I think it is very stupid! If those men are what you say, then they are not good men. They may be very dangerous. I think it better if you leave them alone."

"Well, we can at least keep an eye out for them," Justin said, determination in his voice. "We might discover something the police would listen to."

"Okay," Jenny agreed. "We probably won't even see them,

but we'll keep an eye out. But that's all! If we find out any-thing, we'll tell Uncle Pete. In the meantime, can't we try to have a fun time?"

"What are you kids muttering about?" demanded Uncle Pete.

"Oh, uh . . . nothing important," Justin answered hastily.

He sat up and tried to pay attention to the scenery. Soon he had forgotten the smugglers and was enjoying himself. The road curved, and suddenly Lake Titicaca stretched be-fore them as far as they could see. Circling the horizon, snowcapped mountains peeked at their reflection in the calm, greenish blue water.

"Why, it's as big as an ocean!" Jenny exclaimed.

"It is very big and the highest in the world!" Pedro in-formed them loftily. "Peru is on the other side of the lake. We even have a navy there to watch against Peru."

Copacabana was a sleepy waterside town seemingly trans-ported directly from colonial Spain. Here the green of trees and flowers, fed by the fresh waters of Lake Titicaca, con-trasted with the tans and beiges of the *altiplano*. At Pedro's instruction, Uncle Pete stopped the car two miles from town, and the group scrambled up a steep path to a grassy meadow several hundred feet above the road.

Pedro led them to an enormous flat boulder, its gray sur-face streaked with pale-green lichens. Hacked out of the rock, a series of stone seats faced each other. On the highest part of the boulder, one seat ruled alone over the rest.

"The Tribunal of the Inca," Pedro announced, pointing to the highest seat. "It is said that here a great Inca would sit, judging the quarrels and crimes of my people."

Justin and Jenny had to try out the ancient seats before they left. Hurrying down the path to the car, Justin groaned and clutched his stomach.

"Isn't it about lunch time, Uncle Pete? I'm starving."

"Let's get going then," Uncle Pete ordered. "How about some seafood on the waterfront?"

As Justin opened the back car door, he heard the roar of a powerful engine coming up the road behind them. The twins piled into the back seat as a long, sleek touring car rushed by, leaving them choking in a cloud of dust.

"Well, well!" Justin exclaimed triumphantly, staring after the black car. "If it isn't Skinner and Short!"

"*And* our good friend Pepe," Jenny added.

The black car was lost to sight by the time Uncle Pete started the engine. As they turned into the cobblestone streets of Copacabana, the children gazed down each side street, searching for the black car. Easing the rental car down a steep, narrow street, Uncle Pete pulled up at the waterfront under a sign that announced, *"Restaurant La Cabaña."*

"Hey, guys—look!" Justin pointed across the street to the lake front. A row of wooden piers extended out over the water. Moored alongside the piers, small boats bobbed gently up and down. Pedro and Jenny followed Justin's finger to the wharf, where a black car identical to the one that had passed them sat parked beside the water.

"Come on!" Justin jumped out of the car and hurried toward the wharf. Pedro and Jenny followed more slowly, leaving the astonished Uncle Pete staring after them. As Justin ran out onto the nearest pier, he saw a small motorboat with three familiar men in it moving away toward the green sprinkle of islands in the distance.

The little boat made waves which wet Justin's sneakers as he stood on the end of the pier. He watched the boat disappear around a bend in the shoreline. Thrusting his hands angrily into his pockets, he waited for Pedro and his sister to catch up. "Well, that's that!" he growled.

"What are you kids up to?" Uncle Pete demanded as the three children joined him outside the restaurant.

"We thought we saw someone we knew," Jenny explained quickly.

Uncle Pete raised his eyebrows but dropped the subject. Justin's spirits lifted as he tackled a plate of fresh rainbow trout. It was hard to remember his disappointment when sunshine sparkled through the big picture windows and tiny wooden sailboats danced on the waves below.

"Can I ride in one of those?" Jenny asked as they gathered on the wharf after lunch. They were choosing a boat for their excursion to the Island of the Sun. Gliding up to the pier was a curious craft. Woven from bundles of reeds, it looked like an Eskimo kayak and was large enough to hold just one person.

"Oh, no you don't . . . ," Uncle Pete announced firmly.

"I know what those are," Justin told her. "They're balsa boats, aren't they, Uncle Pete? Made out of reeds that grow in the lake. I read about them in the travel guide."

"That's right, Justin," Uncle Pete answered. "But I think we'll travel in something a bit more up-to-date—like *that* one." He chose a small sailboat with an auxiliary motor and dropped some bills into the smiling owner's hand.

The twins held on tightly to the sides as the sailboat skittered across the waves. Ahead, a small emerald-colored island floated under a cloudless blue sky. In spite of winter temperatures, lush vegetation tumbled down terraced fields still in use after centuries.

The boat docked at the bottom of a wide stone staircase that rose from the water's edge to disappear in a tangle of shrubs far above. Grass forced itself through cracks in the rock, but the staircase was as solid as when slave laborers had built it for Inca emperors a thousand years before.

"Why is this called the Island of the Sun?" Jenny asked Pedro as they climbed the stairs.

"From this island the Sun first rose to shed his light," Pedro told her seriously. "This is the birthplace of the Inca. Here the sun god, *Viracocha,* creator of all, placed the first Inca, *Manco Kapac,* and his woman, *Mama Ocllo,* to bring civilized life to the tribes that lived then on the earth. It is the most sacred of all places to my people."

Justin and Jenny exchanged doubtful glances but didn't argue. At the peak of the island, Pedro guided them through an ancient Inca palace. After making them promise not to leave Pedro, Uncle Pete had stayed behind with the boat owner as guide to explore the island at a slower pace. Justin put Short and Skinner out of his mind. They would be long gone by now.

"You really believe all this stuff, don't you?" Jenny inquired after hearing still another Inca legend.

"You do not believe me?" Pedro asked angrily. "Come, I will show you!" Taking Jenny by the arm, he hurried down an overgrown trail until they stood at the water's edge again. Turning the twins to face the cliff, he indicated a rock formation far above.

"That is the Sacred Rock, the rock where all things began." In the curiously shaped rock were two long, shallow openings, one above the other.

"You see there . . . and there. In the Great Flood that destroyed the world, the Sun and the Moon took refuge there in the sacred rock. All but they were drowned. When the Flood finished, they came out and made life again on the earth. Come!"

Almost running, he hurried them along the waterfront. In the hard limestone that covered the beach were shallow depressions about a yard long, shaped vaguely like giant human footprints.

"See!" Pedro said triumphantly. "There are the footprints of the Sun. The stone was still soft when he rose from the Sacred Rock after the Flood, and his steps were sealed in the stone forever."

"They look like natural rock formations to me," Justin answered skeptically. "So does your 'Sacred Rock'!"

"If you will not believe me, I will tell you no more," Pedro grunted.

"Don't be mad," Jenny pleaded. "You won't believe what we tell you about Jesus, and we don't believe in your sun gods. But we still like hearing your stories, don't we, Justin? Please!"

Responding to Jenny's coaxing, Pedro led them to a mass of ruined buildings just a hundred yards south of the Sacred Rock. A square manmade opening led down into a maze of underground tunnels, but Pedro led them through a series of crumbling rooms to an open courtyard. In the middle of the courtyard was a square altar made of a single block of stone, big enough to hold an ox—or a man.

"Here in *La Chinkana*, sacrifices were made to the Sun," Pedro informed them. "Llamas, sheep, and the most beautiful of the young maidens of my people were given to the Sun for his pleasure."

Jenny shuddered. "How horrible!"

"How can you worship gods who were so cruel?" Justin asked. "They were evil!"

Pedro looked troubled. "The gods are not like men. They do not have to be good. They need only be strong."

"Jesus is good and strong," Jenny insisted. But Pedro only shook his head.

"We promised Uncle Pete we'd be back at the landing at four," Justin said as they came back out into the open. "We'd better not be late again. We've only got an hour before we need to start back."

"Can't we see the underground tunnels?" Jenny asked, turning to Pedro.

"How are you supposed to see in there?" Justin demanded.

"No one must come to the Island of the Sun without seeing the *Laberinto de La Chinkana*," Pedro answered. He reached into his pocket and pulled out a pair of candle stubs and a box of matches. "See? I always am ready."

Outside the opening to the labyrinth, Pedro lit the candle stubs and handed one to Justin. "You must stay close to me. I know the turns needed to come out again. If you do not stay close, you will be lost in the tunnels."

Water dripped from the low roof and walls of the tunnels. The only light was the dim circles of the candles, and black shadows danced on the damp walls just beyond their reach. The smallest sound echoed down the black halls, and the children instinctively lowered their voices to a whisper.

The tunnel twisted right and left, crossing many smaller side passages, until the twins were thoroughly confused. Jenny had just announced she had seen enough when a glow of light appeared only a dozen yards away, down a side tunnel to their right. Instinctively, Justin reached over and knocked Pedro's candle from his hand, blowing out his own in the same instant.

"What did you do that for?" Jenny muttered with annoyance into the dark.

"Shhh! Follow me." Justin whispered as he grabbed for the other two before the light disappeared through another tunnel. As they crept closer to the light that weaved through the darkness, Jenny and Pedro saw what Justin had immediately recognized. The small American, Short, hurried in front of them, carrying a powerful flashlight. At his heels were the massive Skinner and their Latin friend, Pepe.

"They haven't gone after all," Justin whispered. "I'll bet they're on their way to that 'delivery' right now. Come on!"

The three children moved quietly as they followed the men through the maze of tunnels. The slightest sound echoed, but the heavy footsteps of the three men in front of them concealed their own footsteps. The men suddenly stopped at a junction of three tunnels, and the children's own footsteps pattered on several paces before they could come to a halt.

Short pulled what looked like a map from his pocket, but Skinner stared back down the tunnel, the flashlight Short held reflecting a puzzled look on his broad face. The three children pressed back against the wall of the tunnel.

"Did you hear something?" he growled.

Intent on the map he was studying, Short shook his head impatiently. Justin held his breath as Skinner continued staring back down the tunnel for a long moment, trying to pierce the thick darkness that hid the children. Justin's foot began itching, and he felt an almost uncontrollable urge to sneeze.

"I know I heard something!" the big man said at last. "I'm going to check it out!"

"There are always sounds in places like this!" Short snapped. "We don't have time to waste!"

He folded his map, and he and Pepe strode off down the left tunnel, Skinner trailing reluctantly behind. Skinner kept glancing back over his shoulder, but the three children were careful to keep out of sight.

They stopped as the three men descended a short stairway into a wide underground room. There were no other openings into the chamber. In the center of the room, a single candle glowed.

Crouching in the shadows at the top of the stairs, the three children watched as a strange man with the dark, round face and traditional clothing of the Quechua stepped into the candlelight. He carried a small wooden crate.

Pepe greeted the stranger and took the crate. Placing it on the floor, he pulled a screwdriver out of this pocket and proceeded to pry up the lid.

Skinner grunted in approval as he reached into the chest and lifted an object to the light. Then Justin heard his sister gasp softly, and he bit his own lip to stifle a shout. For in the flashlight beam, the object in Skinner's hand shone with the distinct yellow glitter of gold!

Chapter 7

Escape
by Boat

Pedro tugged on Justin's sleeve. "Let us go!" he whispered sharply. "We must leave this place now!"

"Just a minute," Justin whispered back. "I want to see what they're doing." The Indian who had delivered the crate backed into the corner, the flickering candlelight outlining his dark face. Short and his two companions bent over the box, carefully examining its contents.

Lifting a long gold chain to the electric light, Short grunted with satisfaction. He motioned irritably to Skinner, who pulled out his wallet. The delivery man came forward eagerly as Skinner counted out a wad of green bills and thrust them into his hand. Short dropped the chain back into the crate and carefully replaced the lid. Pepe picked up the screwdriver. With the blunt end, he pounded the first nail back into place.

"You are crazy to stay here!" Pedro hissed against Justin's ear. "They will be leaving soon. We will be in great trouble if they find us here. They are very bad men! You may stay here, but I go now!"

"I'm going too," Jenny added firmly. "This is spooky!"

"All right," Justin agreed reluctantly. The three crouching children carefully got to their feet without making a sound. They tiptoed quietly back into the pitch-black of the tunnel, the glow of the flashlight rapidly disappearing behind them.

Only when they had turned two corners, groping their way with one hand on the cold, damp stone of the tunnel wall, did Pedro pull out his box of matches and light the one candle stub they had left.

"We must go quickly!" he said harshly. "You are two very stupid *gringos!* You think this is some game to be played: a great adventure to tell your friends when you go back to your country and your nice, safe home."

The dim glow of the candle reflected the worried anger on his face. "You do not think that there may be real trouble. I have seen this kind of men before. They will kill those who get in their way—and here there is much money to be had. Do you think your kind God will protect you while you play with serpents!"

Pedro set off at a trot, shielding the candle with one hand. He turned right, left, then right again with the ease of someone who had traveled these halls often. Chastened by his words, Justin and Jenny followed meekly. Within minutes they were blinking as their eyes adjusted again to the bright afternoon sun.

Pedro didn't stop at the entrance, but urged them up the hill until they were well hidden by dense shrubs that grew over and around the old stone walls. Justin stopped as Pedro indicated the path that would take them back to the boat landing.

"Just a minute, Pedro. I guess you're right," he said humbly. "I *have* been stupid. I *have* been thinking of this as a great adventure. I never really thought there'd be any danger. I guess it's time we told Uncle Pete and let him handle it."

A triumphant grin split his freckled face as he added, "But we *did* get what we came for, didn't we? We know they really are smugglers, and we've caught them red-handed."

He frowned suddenly. "Now, we just need some proof for the police. We'll have to stay long enough to see where they go next."

Pedro was shaking his head vigorously, his expression still dark with anger. Justin urged, "Come on, Pedro, you don't want them to get away with this, do you? I mean, it's part of this 'Inca heritage' you're so proud of."

"Justin's right!" Jenny interrupted suddenly. "We can't just let them steal all that stuff."

Justin grinned at his sister, then continued, "We'll watch from up here until they come out—just to make sure they've got the stuff with them. Maybe we can see where they store it. The police will have to believe us if we show them where the stuff is hidden. What danger can there possibly be in that?"

After a moment of thought, Pedro nodded reluctantly. "Okay. We watch from here to see where they go. But we watch only. Then we go back to the boat and tell your uncle what has happened."

Pushing through the bushes, Pedro led the twins to a relatively flat spot above the opening to the labyrinth. Taking cover under the thick underbrush, he stretched out on the rough ground and motioned for Justin and Jenny to join him.

As he stretched out beside Pedro, Justin discovered that they had found cover in the middle of a briar patch. He was lying on top of a prickly bramble, and as he shifted position, thorns caught at his hair and clothing. He half-rose to find a more comfortable spot, but Pedro grabbed his arm.

The four men were now emerging from the underground passageway. They moved directly below the children's hiding place so that they were hidden by the overhang of the cliff. The three children could hear the rumble of low voices, but the sounds were too quiet for them to catch more than scattered words of the conversation.

After what seemed a very long wait, the children saw the Indian man move out from beneath the overhang and disappear into the ruins they had explored earlier. The other three men hurried down the path toward the lake. Pepe and Skinner carried the wooden crate, staggering a little under its weight, while Short walked behind them, keeping a sharp eye on the cargo.

"They've got it with them!" Justin muttered triumphantly. Then he added anxiously, "They're climbing down to the beach! They'll get away!"

"Do not worry," Pedro told him. "They cannot get away there unless they swim. There is no landing and no boats."

Pepe and Skinner set down the heavy crate, and the three men moved to the water's edge.

"Don't be so sure!" Justin answered. "Look! What's Skinner got in his hand?"

Skinner had pulled a large whistle out of a pocket. He blew a piercing blast. A few moments later, the motorboat the children had seen carry the men away from the wharf in Copacabana chugged into view. The pilot brought the boat in close to shore. Cutting the engine, he dropped anchor a few yards offshore.

Skinner and Pepe again picked up an end of the crate, and the three men splashed their way toward the boat. Carefully hoisting the crate aboard, they clambered into the boat. The pilot was already gunning the engine, and a moment later, the smugglers and their stolen treasure were lost to view.

"Great!" Justin yelled, his clenched fist striking the ground in frustration. He winced and pulled a thorn from his hand as he added with disgust, "They must have had that boat waiting there the whole time!"

Somehow he'd had the idea that the men would hide their treasure somewhere on the island. He had imagined himself discovering the spot and leading the police victoriously to the treasure.

"We'll never find out what they do with it now!" he said gloomily as he stood up. "And without the gold, the police still won't believe us."

After a pause, he added, "We need more information . . . Look, guys, I know we agreed to get Uncle Pete's help with this mess, but I don't think we can tell him about what we've seen just yet. We need a little more time to think. Agreed?"

Jenny slowly nodded her head. Pedro absently nodded his assent too, as he stared across the beach where waves made by the motorboat still slapped at the shore. His black eyes flashed. "How can men of my own people betray the treasures of our past this way!"

"Well, I suppose some of your people will do anything for money, just like some Americans," Jenny answered.

The three children forced their way back through the briars, stopping to untangle their clothing from the thorns. When they were back on the main path, Justin blew a twig off his watch.

"It's a quarter to four! We'd better get back to the boat landing or Uncle Pete will never let us out alone again."

He started down the path at a run, Pedro and Jenny close behind. Arriving back at the ruined palace, the three hurried down the ancient staircase, two steps at a time. They reached the bottom, panting and out of breath, just as Uncle Pete and his guide walked up to the landing.

"Right on time," was his only comment.

The boat ride back over the dancing blue-green waves was just as beautiful as before, but somehow Justin and Jenny were no longer in the mood for sightseeing. Stepping out at the dock, they walked slowly back to the rental car. All three children piled into the back seat. The twins both rested back against the vinyl seat, not even looking at the spectacular scenery flashing by. Pedro stared moodily out the window.

They had just turned into the outskirts of La Paz when Justin sat up straight, sudden excitement chasing the gloom from his face.

"Jenny," he demanded in a voice too low for anyone else to hear, "if you were those guys, where would you take that stuff next?"

Jenny was tired of the whole affair. "I don't know!" she answered crossly. "Anywhere, I guess."

"Not just anywhere. You see, we know something about them no one else does. *We know where they're staying!*"

"You mean, their hotel room?" Jenny asked. "Don't be crazy! They'd never go back there—not when they know we're on to them."

"But that's the whole point! They *don't* know we're on to them. They didn't see us at the digging site, and I'm sure Pepe hasn't said anything about meeting us . . . not after the way he hurried us out of there. They can't possibly know we were watching them on the island. As far as they know, we're just dumb tourists."

His eyebrows knit together as he thought. "Now, if we could just get a look inside their room . . ."

"You promised to let Uncle Pete handle it," Jenny protested.

"We will. But it'd make more sense for us to take a peek at their room first. Then he'd have something to tell the police."

Pedro continued to stare out the window, and Justin didn't think he had overheard their whispered conversation. He was sure the other boy wouldn't approve. When they arrived back at their hotel, Uncle Pete dropped them off at the front door.

"I need to take the car back, then I have a short business appointment. Restaurants don't open around here until about eight o'clock. I should be back by then, and we'll get something to eat. Mr. Evans mentioned a good pizza place around the corner. If you kids want something to do, maybe you'd like to walk down to the market with Pedro. You've never seen anything like the open-air market here."

"No, thanks, Uncle Pete," Justin answered politely. "Uh . . . I think we'll just stay here at the hotel and rest. Right, Jenny? It's been a long day, and we're really tired. Pedro is probably tired too. It'd be nice if he could have the rest of the day off."

Uncle Pete raised his eyebrows, obviously surprised to hear his energetic relatives admitting fatigue. "Fine, I'll meet you back here then," he agreed. "I suppose you're not quite used to the altitude yet. Just don't go wandering off alone!"

Pedro stared at them suspiciously, as though wondering what the two were up to. "I be here first thing tomorrow," he said at last. "You not make any trouble, okay?"

When Uncle Pete and Pedro were gone, Justin and Jenny hurried into the wide lobby. As usual, the clerk was gone.

Justin suspected that he spent most of his time taking a *siesta* in the back room. He checked the boxes.

"They're not here yet. Their key is still in the box." Reaching over the counter, he pulled down the key to his room. "Come on. We'll sit quietly in my room. That way we'll be able to hear them when they come in, and they won't know we're here. Once they get here, we'll find out if they still have the treasure."

"*If* they get here," Jenny muttered. "Anyway, they'll check just like we did. When they see your key is missing from the box, they'll know we're back."

"You're right." Opening the small gate that led behind the counter, Justin groped around on a knee-high shelf.

"I saw him put it here yesterday. Ah ha, here it is!" He held up an extra room key and slipped it into the empty box.

Upstairs, Justin and Jenny stretched out quietly on Justin's bed, Jenny still unhappy at what she considered a complete waste of time. Whenever she opened her mouth to give her opinion of the whole idea, Justin whispered, "Shhh!" So they waited in silence in the slowly darkening room.

They had almost fallen asleep when they heard heavy footsteps on the stairs and the rattle of a key. The door of the next room slammed shut. A deep voice growled something they couldn't make out, and a higher one answered. Justin sat up and jumped off the bed.

"It's them! Come on."

Jenny grabbed at the back of Justin's jacket. "Are you crazy?" she hissed. "You can't just barge in on them! Pedro's right. We could get hurt doing this!"

Justin flushed. "Sorry!" he mumbled apologetically. "I guess we'd better wait until they've gone."

He sat back down. The minutes stretched like years as the

room next door settled into quiet. Only an occasional murmur of voices told the two children that someone was still there. The sun's late afternoon rays lengthened and dimmed, and finally disappeared altogether. But they didn't dare turn on the light.

The twins had just decided the smugglers had settled in for the night when they heard the door open and several pair of heavy footsteps stomp out onto the balcony. The door slammed shut again, and there was the barely audible sound of a key turning in the lock. Justin and Jenny waited without moving until all was quiet on the balcony once more. Then Justin moved quietly to the window and lifted the curtain to peer out.

"I don't see anyone! Let's go."

He reached under the bed and pulled a small disposable flashlight out of his suitcase. His camera still hung around his neck, and he checked it for film. Motioning to his sister, he opened the door a crack. Jenny peered over his shoulder. The balcony was empty. Slipping out onto the balcony, they checked the courtyard below. No one was in sight. Jenny tried the knob of the next room.

"It's locked!" she said shortly. "Now what are we going to do?"

Justin produced the key to their room. "Watch!"

He slipped the key into the lock and jiggled it back and forth. When he heard a faint click, he turned the key. Justin grinned triumphantly as he swung the door inward.

"I mistook this door for mine our first day here," he explained. "That's when I found out these keys will open any door in the hotel with a little work."

The twins slipped through the open door, then Justin locked it behind them. Not until then did he flick the switch of his flashlight. He inhaled sharply at the sight that met his eyes.

In the center of the room stood a small, round table. On the table, still in the wooden crate, a treasure trove of riches glittered under the thin beam of the flashlight. Spellbound, the two children stepped closer. Justin moved his flashlight back and forth over the contents of the crate.

Golden bracelets and necklaces set with strange green stones, glinted up at them. Tiny silver statues of llamas and condors—the sacred bird of the Inca—lay against menacing figures that reminded Justin of the strange faces in the Underground Temple of Tiawanaku.

Jenny reached out slowly and picked up a figure that reminded her of the monolith she had seen of *Pacha Mama*. It fit snugly into the palm of her hand, and she ran a finger over the cool smoothness of the gold.

Placed carefully on top was the most wonderful piece of all: a six-inch balsa boat of pure gold, an exact miniature copy of those they had seen that afternoon. An Inca prince stood in the center of the boat, his arms folded across his chest. His proud features were perfectly formed. A feathered cloak worked in exquisite detail was flung over his shoulder. In the bow of the boat, a naked rower held his paddle high as he waited through the centuries for his master's orders.

"He's beautiful!" Jenny whispered in awe.

Justin handed the flashlight to Jenny and raised his camera to his eye. The brilliance of the flash lit the room as he took two shots of the golden treasure. Jenny turned the flashlight on the tiny figure of *Pacha Mama* for a closer look. So engrossed were they that neither heard the click of a key in the lock.

Suddenly, the door slammed open and the light snapped

on. Startled, Justin shoved his camera into his pocket as Skinner lunged into the room, his broad face ugly with anger.

"It's those kids!" Short and Pepe crowded into the room after him as Skinner quickly checked through the open crate of treasure. Instinctively, Jenny shut her hand tightly over the small gold figure she held.

The angry giant took a step toward the two children. "What do you think you're doing here?" he shouted.

Justin and Jenny stepped backward, but Skinner kept advancing on the frightened children until they were backed tight against the wall. Jenny pressed close to Justin as Skinner's heavy fists clenched and unclenched with rage.

"Answer me!" he bellowed threateningly.

Justin's hands were trembling, but his voice was almost steady as he answered, "Uh, we were coming by . . . and we saw your souvenirs . . . They were so beautiful . . . we just had to take a closer look at them."

The two children crept along the wall toward the door. "Look, I'm awfully sorry we bothered your stuff," Justin added politely. "We just wanted to look. We'll leave you alone now. My uncle's waiting for us."

Short walked up to the children. He was smiling, but Justin shuddered as he got closer. "So you just happened by, did you? You just happened to open a locked door. For some reason, you didn't bother to turn on the light."

He looked at the flashlight in Jenny's shaking fingers. "You just happened to be carrying that, eh? And what else do you have?"

The smile suddenly disappeared as he grabbed Jenny's wrist and twisted it. The tiny figure of *Pacha Mama* fell to the floor.

"I'm afraid you two aren't going anywhere!" he continued as softly as a rattlesnake sliding across a rock. "You've got some explaining to do. Pepe, the door!"

Pepe reached behind him and the lock clicked. As the three men advanced toward them, Justin and Jenny stared at each other in dismay. They were trapped, and they could see no way out!

Chapter 8

Trapped
By Smugglers

"*L*et's see how much you know," Short said, still speaking softly.

He gave Skinner a quick nod. An unpleasant grin of enjoyment spread across the big man's face. Jenny was still clutching the flashlight, and she quickly shoved it into her jeans pocket just as Skinner grabbed both twins by the back of the neck and half-dragged them across the room.

Justin and Jenny twisted and turned, but Skinner's broad, meaty hands were iron-strong. Chuckling at their attempts to break loose, the big man shoved the two children onto a bed and loomed over them. Grabbing Justin by a handful of red curls, he shoved his face so close that Justin almost choked at the sour odor of his breath.

"You tell me what you two are doing here or I'm going to get real mean!" he demanded roughly.

Jenny jumped up from the bed. "Get your hands off my brother!"

Skinner's thick lips spread into a nasty grin as he turned

his attention to the girl. "Well, well! Is Mommy afraid her baby will get hurt?"

Releasing Justin, he shoved Jenny so hard that she fell back across the bed. Then he turned his attention back to Justin, yanking his head back until Justin was sure his hair was coming out by the roots.

"If you don't want anyone hurt, you'd better start talking. I'll bet you two were our little spies yesterday out at the diggings, weren't you?" His grin grew wider with satisfaction as he read the answer in Justin's startled face.

"Okay, who else knows about this?" he growled, his voice deep and threatening. "Did you tell your uncle about your little treasure hunt?"

Skinner sounded so much like a "bad guy" in some old cowboy movie that Justin suddenly lost his fear. A slow anger began to burn within him as he stared unblinkingly up at the big man.

"Uncle Pete doesn't know anything about this!" he answered defiantly. "You'd better let us go right now! Someone's going to be looking for us pretty soon, and you're going to be in a lot of trouble if you don't let us go!"

Skinner let go of Justin's hair, shaking his head slowly as he thought about the boy's words. His broad, ugly face suddenly looked worried and unhappy.

"You really didn't tell anyone about us?" he asked uncertainly, running a hand through the strip of hair that crossed his shaved head.

"Of course we didn't!" he answered. "We were just looking around . . . the way kids do."

Justin rubbed the back of his neck, wincing as he felt the marks of Skinner's fingers. *This guy really isn't very smart,* he thought.

Skinner hunched his massive shoulders and scratched his chin, thinking hard. "Well, I guess you can go . . . if you promise you won't tell anyone!"

"Are you out of your mind?" Short paced across the room and elbowed Skinner aside. "Let me handle this, you idiot!"

He cuffed Justin across the side of the head. "You think you're really smart, don't you, kid? We warned you about snooping around. Now you know more than is good for you, so I'm afraid you'll have to stay right here."

Jenny jumped to her feet again. "You'd better let us go!" she challenged bravely, but with a shakiness in her voice. "Uncle Pete is looking for us by now. You can't get away with keeping us here."

Short's narrow, weasel-like face held no expression, but something about the cold, pale-blue eyes made Justin swallow in sudden fear. Here, Justin suddenly realized, was the boss of the smuggling operation.

"You lie!" Short said flatly. "We've already checked through the building, and you two are the only ones here. In any case . . . Skinner, get downstairs and keep a lookout for anyone coming in. See if you can handle that, at least, without blowing it!"

He motioned to Pepe. "You! Get these two tied up and lock them in the bathroom. Gag 'em too." He handed Pepe a roll of thin nylon rope.

Pepe, his brown eyes faintly apologetic, pushed the two children into the bathroom. Pulling Justin's arms behind his back, he tied them tightly, then stretched the long length of rope over to tie Jenny's hands. There was little room to sit on the tiny bathroom floor, so he shoved the twins into the curtainless shower stall and pushed them to the floor.

"I am sorry," he told them in a low voice as he wound the

rope around their ankles. "Did I not tell you to get away? Why did you come back?"

"I guess . . . I guess we were just playing a game," Justin answered slowly, remembering Pedro's accusation. He looked thoughtfully at Pepe. "You seem nice. You aren't really going to help them get away with this, are you?"

"Please let us go!" Jenny pleaded.

Pepe shook his head sadly. "I am sorry. I wish I could help, but they will kill me if I allow your escape."

Avoiding their eye, he reached for one of the bed sheets and tore off two strips of cloth. Gagging them securely, he left the room without looking back, swinging the door closed behind him.

When he had gone, Justin quietly tested the strength of his bonds. Pepe had left the light off, and the gags prevented the twins from talking. Justin tugged at the ropes until his wrists ached, but Pepe had tied them securely. He finally quit trying, realizing that they couldn't get by the men in the other room even if they did get loose.

Leaning back against the shower stall, he shut his eyes wearily and tried to concentrate on a plan of escape. Occasionally he caught the murmur of voices in the other room, but the men spoke too quietly for him to make out words. Beside him, Jenny lay on her side motionless, and Justin thought she must be asleep.

Justin couldn't tell how much time had passed before he opened his eyes again. He only knew that his hands and feet had lost all feeling. The rest of his body ached enough to make up for them, though. He glanced around the darkness, then sat up with a start as he caught a glimpse of Pepe leaning over an open suitcase.

He stared, confused, then realized what had happened.

When Pepe swung the door shut earlier, the latch hadn't caught. Now the door had opened slightly. In a full-length mirror on the bathroom wall Justin now had a clear view of part of the other room, including the locked door.

He watched Pepe's reflection snap a suitcase shut and place it beside the door. Then Short moved into Justin's field of vision, carrying another suitcase. On the table, the chest of stolen treasure still winked at him, but as he watched, Pepe replaced the lid and picked up a hammer. The smugglers were obviously moving out.

A key rattled in the lock, and Skinner stomped in. "There ain't no one down there!" he growled. "Are you guys about ready to go? I've got the car ready and waiting."

Just then, Justin heard quick footsteps along the balcony, and a sharp knock sounded at the door. The three men froze. "Sure there's no one down there!" Short snapped. "Skinner, can't you do anything right?"

The big man shrugged helplessly as another knock was heard and a loud voice called out. Justin straightened up with a jerk, and Jenny struggled to a sitting position as they recognized the voice that spoke. Uncle Pete had found them at last! Now, if they could only get his attention!

Striding over to the door, Short opened it just enough to peer out. Justin kept his eyes glued to the faint reflection, grinning with delight under the gag as Uncle Pete's deep voice boomed, "Have you seen anything of a girl and a boy—thirteen-year-old twins?"

Standing in the doorway to prevent Uncle Pete from seeing into the room, Short answered, "As a matter of fact, we did see a couple of kids. American, right?"

He turned to Skinner. "You remember those kids we passed down the street, don't you? A redheaded boy and a girl. I noticed them because they were chattering away in English."

"Yeah," Skinner's gravelly voice added. "Toward the market, that's where they were heading."

Oh, no! He's going to believe them! Justin thought desperately. *I've got to make some noise!*

Raising his heels as far into the air as he could, he let them bang to the floor. The resulting thump echoed in the tiny bathroom, and he repeated it. Jenny too, catching on to what Justin was trying to do, thumped her heels against the wall.

"What's going on in there?" Uncle Pete demanded. Justin caught sight of a full red beard as Uncle Pete pushed through the doorway. Justin went limp with relief. *He'll find us after all,* he thought.

Then he saw Short nod to Pepe. Pepe picked up the hammer and began pounding in nails on the crate lid. Short opened the door wide and said loudly, "Oh, that's just Pepe, finishing up some packing. We have a late plane to catch tonight. Now, if you're through looking around . . ."

Justin and Jenny doubled their efforts, but Pepe's hammering drowned out the faint sound. Uncle Pete's exasperated words rang out over their noise. "Well, if they show up here before you leave, please let them know their uncle is looking for them. And tell them to stay put here at the hotel!"

"We'll give 'em the message, mister," Short promised, beaming with fatherly kindness as he ushered Uncle Pete out the door. "Don't you worry any. Kids are like that, always running off. They'll turn up safe and sound."

The twins heard Uncle Pete thank them. As he watched the door slam shut behind his uncle, Justin groaned inwardly. If only they had told Uncle Pete about this mess before! Now no one knew where they were, and their last chance of rescue was gone.

The bathroom door opened and Short stepped in. He slapped them both, hard. "That'll teach you not to make noise!"

His ears ringing from the blow, Justin glared at Short over his gag. Short leaned down with a knife and slashed the ropes at their ankles. "You've got some walking to do," he informed the two children, yanking them to their feet. But their legs, now completely numb, wouldn't hold them, and they collapsed again to the floor.

Impatiently, Short slashed the ropes on their wrists as well. "You've got five minutes to rub some life into those legs. Now move!"

He left the bathroom. Angry tears welled up in Jenny's brown eyes as she rubbed at her legs with almost useless hands. Justin reached over and patted her awkwardly, his eyes above the gag trying to convey his sympathy. Jenny nodded back and brushed the tears away, and both children turned back to rubbing. Painful prickles soon replaced the numbness as feeling returned to their limbs.

A few minutes later Pepe entered and helped them into the other room. Justin looked around. Dressers and closets stood open and empty. The packed suitcases were piled neatly beside the door. The wooden crate, its lid now nailed back on, still lay on the table. Short stood beside it, counting out bills from an open wallet.

Skinner lifted a pair of suitcases. "I'll go load up. Where do we go next, Short?"

"We've got that last load to pick up at Tiawanaku. We'll have to drag the kids along for now. For sure, we can't come back here again. We'll be out of the country by tomorrow anyway."

"Yeah, and I suppose we'll have to find a truck now and head south for the Argentine border," Skinner growled. "After we had your buddy's private plane all arranged!"

Satisfied with the contents of his wallet, Short shoved it back into his pocket and replied sharply, "We'll be on that plane tomorrow just like we planned."

"But, Short, they know who we are now. And they'll be watching every airport in the country once we turn the kids loose."

"*Who* knows who we are?" Short answered smoothly. "You heard these kids say they didn't tell anyone else. They are the only witnesses against us—the only ones between us and freedom. You aren't planning on letting two kids get in our way, are you, Skinner?"

Justin grew cold with terror as the two men turned and looked at them, Skinner with sudden cruel pleasure, Short with the flat, unwinking stare of a rattlesnake preparing to strike.

Turning away, Short commanded, "Pepe, get the kids something to eat and drink before we go. The coffee's all ready over there. And hurry up. We've got to get out of here before their uncle shows up again."

Picking up a pair of suitcases, he headed out the door. Skinner followed, leaving the two children alone with Pepe. The kinky-haired Spaniard looked strangely pale under his dark tan as he fumbled with their gags. His hands trembled so much that he finally had to resort to a knife to cut the knots.

"Hold still or I cut you!" he warned.

Justin spit out the grimy rag. His mouth was so dry he could hardly swallow. "Please!" he croaked. "A drink of water!"

Pepe shook his head and brought them each a piece of bread and a cup of black coffee. They gulped the hot coffee eagerly, but he snatched the cups away after one swallow and handed them the bread.

"No more!" he whispered. "It is bad coffee! Now remember, no matter what, pretend you are asleep!"

Before he could say more, Short and Skinner re-entered the room. Glancing nervously in their direction, Pepe carried the cups into the bathroom, and the children heard the sound of running water.

Justin managed only a few bites of bread before he began feeling strangely dizzy. Beside him, Jenny dropped her bread to the floor. "I feel awful!" she whispered.

Shaking his head to clear it, Justin helped his sister to a bed. As he collapsed down beside her, he saw Short watching them with satisfaction. Justin thrust his hands into his jacket pockets to keep them from shaking. One hand encountered the camera he had shoved in there earlier, but the other touched something sharp. It was the piece of pottery he had found in the ruins the day before.

He glanced around quickly. Short and Skinner were now bent over what looked like a road map, arguing in low voices. Hardly aware of what he was doing, he pulled the clay shard from his pocket and thrust it under the mattress.

Pepe hurried back into the room. Yanking Justin and Jenny to their feet, he grabbed both children by an arm and hurried them to the stairs. Justin was finding it difficult to concentrate on where he was going. His head spun, and each step dragged as though he were walking in quicksand. He vaguely sensed Jenny stumbling along beside him.

As he tumbled into the back of the long, black car, he managed to mutter, "It was the coffee! They drugged the coffee!" But no one heard him, and he and Jenny were already sound asleep.

Chapter 9

Cave of the Inca Rey

Justin awoke to the bumping of a moving car. *Where am I?* he wondered. *What am I doing in this car?* As he lay quietly, a voice echoed in his mind, "Remember, pretend you are asleep!"

The events of the past few hours came rushing back. *The coffee*, he remembered. Pepe had given them coffee, and they had fallen asleep. Justin guessed the coffee had been meant to put them out for many hours. But Pepe had allowed them only a swallow, just enough to fool the children's captors.

Good old Pepe, Justin thought gratefully.

Was Jenny awake too? He reached out in the dark and squeezed her hand. She squeezed back, but she too lay as though she were asleep.

The car pulled to a stop and the three men climbed out. One leaned through the open window and shone a bright light into the back seat, but Justin and Jenny kept their eyes shut and breathed lightly, as though sleeping. The light moved away, and Short's high voice directed, "They're still out! Let's get the stuff and get out of here!"

Justin lay still until the sound of the retreating footsteps died away, then he cautiously lifted his head to the window. A full moon shone on tumble-down stone walls. He touched his sister on the shoulder. "We're at Tiawanaku. Let's go! This is our only chance to escape!"

Justin started to open the car door but stopped. "No, wait . . . they'll see the dome light." Seeing the window down, he scrambled over the seat and climbed out, sliding quietly to the ground. Jenny did the same. On hands and knees, they carefully crawled around to the other side of the car. The cold night air of the thirteen-thousand-feet-high plain blew away the last of their drug-induced sleep.

Raising his head slowly, Justin peered across the hood of the car into the night. There was no sign of their captors. Nor was there sign of any living soul. The guards and local Indians who peddled merchandise and fake artifacts to tourists had returned to their villages for the night.

Crouching now beside the car, Justin patted his jacket and discovered his camera was still there. The smugglers hadn't taken the time to search them. He turned to Jenny. "Do you still have the flashlight?"

Jenny pulled the small flashlight from a jeans pocket. "Yes, it's right here."

Justin stopped her before she could switch it on. "Not now! They might see the light. We don't need it anyway."

He pointed toward the full moon that floated serenely above them. The flat plain, touched with silver by the moonlight, stretched around them for miles, offering little opportunity to hide.

"We'll have to try the ruins," Justin whispered. "It's the only place that isn't in the open."

They began running up the slight incline toward the safe walls of Tiawanaku. There was no way to escape the bright, revealing light of the moon. As they reached the wire fence that cut the ruins off from the road, Justin glanced back. His heart sank as he saw a massive shadow move from behind the small concrete building where they had bought tickets the day before. An angry shout told the twins the men had seen them.

Justin pushed frantically on the gate that opened into the ruins before he noticed the heavy iron padlock. "We'll have to climb over!" Jenny whispered loudly. But Justin was already scrambling up the heavy mesh of the gate. The strands of barbwire that ran along the top of the fence were missing here. At the top, he reached down a hand for Jenny.

The two children climbed over the gate, dropped to the ground, and ran. Seconds later they heard a heavy body slam against the wire fence only a hundred yards behind them. As a flashlight beam pierced the night, searching for the twins, they continued to run, chests heaving from the scant oxygen of the high plateau.

When they reached the outer wall of the main temple complex, Jenny collapsed against the rough granite, struggling to catch her breath. "I'm so . . . tired!" she panted. "I can't . . . run anymore!"

"You've got to!" Justin whispered fiercely. "They're coming!"

Following his pointing finger, Jenny recognized the heavy bulk of Skinner and the slighter shadow of Short. The sharp report of a gun burst the silence, and a moment later the gate swung open.

"They shot off the lock!" Justin hissed. "We've got to get out of here!" He grabbed Jenny's hand again, and the two began to run along the high stone wall. They paused at the foot of a narrow staircase that led up into the main temple complex, but as they caught the flicker of a light at the far end of the wall, they turned and ran up the stone steps.

Ghostly black silhouettes dotted the moonlit grass carpet of the vast temple courtyard. Pointing at the far side of the courtyard, Justin whispered, "If we can climb down that wall and get into those ruins over there, they'll never find us."

But before they had a chance to move, they saw a beam of light float up the steps they had just climbed. Justin quickly pulled his sister behind one of the stone monoliths. Peering around the crumbling block of granite, he waited. He breathed a sigh of relief as the light moved behind the low stone wall that ran half the length of the courtyard.

Suddenly he froze as Short's high, thin voice echoed, seemingly inches away. Jenny tensed beside him. The twins hardly dared breathe as Short grumbled loudly, "Where did those stupid kids go? You should have known they'd be waking up soon!"

"It's your own fault!" Skinner's deeper voice whined. "You said those drops would knock them out for hours."

Justin's eyes roamed the darkness behind them. Careful not to make a sound, he again peered around the granite figure. He was puzzled not to see any sign of the two smugglers, but Short's high tones rang out once more. "Never mind! If they get back to the police, we've both had it. I'll check in here. You go around the other side."

Justin suddenly remembered the age-old loudspeaker set into the stone not far from the staircase they had just climbed. The two smugglers must be standing directly behind the stone loudspeaker at the far end of the low wall that divided the courtyard.

Jenny echoed his thoughts in a whisper. "They're behind the wall. They can't see us!"

"But we can't get back to the wall and down into the ruins," Justin whispered back. "They'd catch us for sure. We'll have to go down the front steps."

The beam of light suddenly moved from behind the stone wall. "Come on!" Justin whispered urgently. Staying in the safety of the shadows, the two children slipped from the shelter of one giant monolith to the next, always moving toward the main temple entrance. Once, Justin almost cried out as a round, unearthly face loomed above them. He pulled Jenny to a stop before he recognized *Pacha Mama*, the "Mother Earth" that Pedro had pointed out the day before.

The *Pacha Mama* was the last of the granite monoliths between them and the entrance, and Justin suddenly realized that a wide expanse of open ground lay ahead of them. As he paused uncertainly, a cloud drifted over the moon. Taking advantage of the sudden shadow, the two children made a dash for the wide gateway of the temple and hurried down the broad steps.

The Semisubterranean Temple spread out before them like a submerged swimming pool. As they trotted across the ancient paving stones, the moon broke out again from behind its covering. Its ghostly light outlined the strange carved faces that lined the underground walls, their sightless eyes watching over the vast ruins of the city as they had for centuries.

"We'll have to go that way," he whispered, pointing across the pool to the open fields they had explored the day before. "There aren't many hiding places, but there are houses across the field. We can get help there."

"Those houses are only mud huts!" Jenny objected. "Besides, those Indians won't understand anything we say. And we saw some of those men helping Short and Skinner. How do we know they won't turn us over to them?"

"Do you have a better idea? We can't stay here! If we can get into the hills where they were digging, there's lots of places to hide."

They had almost reached the open fields when Jenny caught her foot in a tangled plant and fell forward, the breath knocked out of her in a loud gasp of pain. The twins froze for a moment, hoping no one had heard Jenny's cry. But seconds later they heard running feet.

"They're over your way!" Short's high voice shouted. It sounded very near. "Get them!"

Justin glanced back. A beam of light bobbed to their left, cutting them off from the open fields. Grabbing Jenny's hand, Justin turned toward the long, evenly shaped mound that loomed close ahead. Jenny pulled on her brother's arm. "Not that way! You're going toward the cave!"

"We've . . . got no . . . choice!" Justin panted out, running faster. "We'll have to go . . . over the top!" But as the two children reached the mound, they slid to a stop in dismay. Stepping out from behind the massive building blocks that grave robbers had left piled at the foot of the mound, Skinner appeared, turned up the corners of his thick lips in gloating satisfaction.

The big man chuckled hoarsely as he walked forward, his great bulk blocking their escape. Behind them, Short played his flashlight over their motionless figures. There was only one way open. "Come on," Justin whispered. Before the two men could move, Justin and Jenny were scrambling straight up the steep hillside toward the *Cueva de la Inca Rey.*

Justin had planned to climb to the top of the mound and try to lose the smugglers in the tumbled granite blocks on the other side, but as they reached the piled-up boulders that blocked the entrance of the cave, he pulled Jenny to a stop.

"In there!" he hissed, motioning toward the ragged opening, dark against the hillside.

Jenny stared at him in horror. "We can't go in there! We'll be killed! Don't you remember what Pedro said?"

Justin glanced back down the hillside. The two smugglers were only steps behind. "Yes, we can," he answered urgently, squeezing through the tight break in the brick wall. "God will protect us. Besides, there's nowhere else to go!"

Jenny tumbled in behind him, and he pulled her down beside him just as Skinner thrust his head through the opening. The two children backed away as the big man tried to force his way in. He swore viciously as his bulky shoulders jammed in the opening.

"Get out of the way, idiot, and let *me* in!" Short ordered coldly. Skinner moved away with a loud tear of ripping cloth. Justin held his breath as Short peered in, until he saw that the crumbled opening was too tight even for the smaller man. Outside, curses filled the air as Skinner pounded against the bricks with his bare fists.

"Don't be stupid!" the two children heard Short hiss.

"We'll never reach them that way!"

Ignoring them, Justin put an arm around his sister, who was now shaking with cold and fear. Pressing his other hand to his aching side, he leaned his head back against the wall. Jenny groped for his hand.

"I'm so scared!" she sobbed.

"Let's pray," Justin whispered back, his own lips trembling. "Only God can help us now!"

Chapter 10

Lost in the Labyrinth

The cursing and banging outside had died away. It was very quiet inside the cave, very dark, and very, very cold. Though the sun warmed it during the day, the *altiplano* dipped below freezing at night. A strong gust of wind whistled through the small opening in the wall, biting into their thin jackets. Backing away from the draft, Justin thought with longing of his heavy down coat back at the hotel.

Jenny huddled against him, still shivering. "Do you think they'll come back? Maybe we should get out of here while we have a chance."

"We're safer in here than out there right now," Justin said bluntly.

Jenny was silent for a moment. "Justin, do you believe that story of Pedro's . . . about the curse of the Inca? Do you think something will happen to us for coming in here?"

"I don't know whether I believe it or not, but it doesn't matter," he answered. "Remember what Uncle Pete said— the power of God is stronger than any curse. He will protect us!"

"I . . . I know. But I'm still afraid."

A sudden crash broke the silence of the cave. "Okay, kids," bellowed Skinner's hoarse voice. "You come out of there or we're coming in after you. And if we have to come in, it'll be the worse for you!"

The two children scrambled to their feet. They froze as another crash sent a shower of broken bricks scattering across the cave. The thin beam of moonlight widened as a section of the wall caved in.

"They've got pickaxes!" Justin exclaimed. "Come on! We can't let them catch us!"

The full moon poured through the wider opening, turning the darkness into gray shadow. The twins could now make out the dim outline of their surroundings. They were in an immense vaulted chamber. The vast room was empty of furnishings, but deep shadows here and there offered promise of shelter.

The moon's silver turned to gold as a hairy, muscular arm lifted a flashlight through the opening. In its light the children saw that the shadows around the chamber were caused by archways of various sizes. Strange carvings filled the spaces in-between.

"They're coming in!" Justin whispered urgently. "We've got to hide!"

The twins ran across the stone blocks that paved the floor and ducked into a small archway that was about three feet wide. They pressed backward into the darkness but had only taken two steps when they felt a wall at their backs. Justin groped for another opening, but only discovered more carvings.

Further blows of the pickax reverberated like thunder in

the cave. A final crash toppled a whole section of the brick wall, then they heard a scrambling as the smugglers climbed through the gap.

"Nothing in here!" they heard Skinner grumble in disappointment as a beam of light pierced the darkness of their hiding place.

"We're here for the kids, not treasure!" Short shouted. They've got to be hidden somewhere. Search every one of those openings until you find them!"

The two children inched forward and peered out cautiously. The smugglers were on the far side of the room, Skinner's flashlight probing each archway. There was no sign of Pepe. Justin wondered if he had seized the chance to make his own escape.

The powerful beam slowly circled in their direction. "We've got to get out of here!" Justin whispered urgently. "We'll be trapped!"

"Let's try a bigger archway!" Jenny whispered back. "They may go further in."

Slipping away, Justin and Jenny crept through the shadows until they found the next opening. This arch was as wide as a doorway and reached far overhead. Holding hands, they stepped through the archway. This time their groping hands felt only empty space ahead and rough stone walls to each side. They were in some sort of passageway.

Creeping along the wall until they were beyond the reach of the smugglers' light, the two children stopped and waited breathlessly as a light played across the archway, paused momentarily, then passed on.

"Those kids aren't anywhere!" they heard Skinner shout. "They must have gotten back out!"

"They've passed us!" Justin whispered with relief. "Now

we just have to wait till they leave."

But a moment later, the light beam moved back across the opening. This time it stopped, probing the darkness deeply. Then, to their shock, the twins watched the circle of light enter the tunnel.

"No, those kids are still in here!" Short's high, expressionless words echoed off the stone walls. "Let's take a look down here."

The twins inched backward as Short and Skinner moved quickly along the passageway. The approaching light illuminated other tunnels leading off on both sides of the passageway. Justin and Jenny ducked into the nearest opening just as the circle of light swept over them.

"Something moved down there!" Skinner rumbled.

"We know you're there, kids!" Short shouted. "You might as well give up!"

"What do we do now?" Jenny whispered in panic.

"We'll have to go further in," Justin answered. "Come on!"

"But we'll get lost!" Jenny protested. "We'd never find our way out of all these tunnels."

Justin thought frantically. The heavy footsteps of the two men were approaching rapidly and would soon reach their new hiding place.

"I've got it!" he whispered. Reaching into his jacket pocket, he pulled out the small stone he had used as chalk in the ruins the day before.

"We'll mark our way with this," he told his sister, rubbing the light-colored stone against the darker stone of the tunnel wall. The edge crumbled away slightly, but it left a clear mark beside the tunnel entrance.

"Once we lose them, we'll trace our way back with the

flashlight. You've still got it, don't you?"

As she nodded, he broke into a run, pulling Jenny after him—just as the footsteps paused outside their hiding place. His free hand located another opening to his left, and he ducked inside.

Jenny hung back. "But won't they just see the marks and follow us?"

"Do you have a better idea?" Justin snapped back. "Besides, how would they know they're *our* marks?"

He scratched a mark beside the archway, his makeshift chalk crumbling even further as he did so.

"Maybe they won't look in here!" he told her as they backed into the darkness.

But it wasn't long before they again heard approaching footsteps. The twins hurried down this new tunnel as the beam of light entered their hiding place. They noticed that the passageway slanted downhill. Soon they were almost running as the incline grew steeper. The glow of the light behind them kept them from stumbling, and the heavy footsteps of the smugglers drowned out the sound of their own running feet.

The tunnel ended in a junction, and the two children lunged into the left passageway, Justin pausing to mark the tunnel they had just left. Then they grabbed hands again and ran blindly into the inky blackness ahead.

Jenny's outstretched arm found the next opening. Once inside, they could no longer see or hear any sign of their pursuers, and they dropped to the tunnel floor to rest. *There's something familiar about this place*, Justin thought as he leaned back against the stone wall.

Then he remembered the labyrinth they had explored with Pedro only that afternoon. Perhaps the same Inca architect had designed this similar maze of tunnels. But where those walls had oozed dampness, this place was as dry as the desert above. The air was still and heavy, and no longer as cold this far from the main entrance.

"Doesn't this remind you of the Island of the Sun?" Jenny asked, echoing his thoughts.

Before Justin could answer, a dim glow appeared against the entrance of the passageway where they rested. He made a quick motion.

"Aren't they ever going to leave us alone?" he whispered savagely, jumping up and pulling Jenny to her feet. They began to run again, ducking into side tunnels and changing direction every few minutes. Yet the beam of light and the echoing footsteps followed them stubbornly.

The passageways continued to slope downward, and Justin guessed they must be well underground by now. At each turn he paused to mark on the wall, the white scrapes faintly visible in the weak beam of the flashlight far behind them. The twins grew to hate that light with a passion as the deadly game of hide and seek went on.

They had changed direction so often that Justin knew they could never find their way back to the surface on their own. But by now his makeshift piece of chalk was almost crumbled away. They would have to stop soon or risk losing their way in the endless maze of tunnels.

The twins had turned into yet another passageway when Jenny dropped to the tunnel floor, unable to go further. She bent over, wheezing. "I can't . . . breathe!" she gasped. "I'm suffocating! Oh, Justin . . . do you think it's . . . the curse?"

Justin reached out in the dark to take her hand. "God won't let the curse hurt us, Jenny!" Just then a familiar glow moved into view, and the two children struggled to their feet once more.

"I wish God would do something about the smugglers!" Jenny muttered as they stumbled on.

By now they were too tired to move fast, and the persistent beam slowly gained on them. Its increasing light revealed that this passageway was much wider and higher than the others. To the twins' dismay, there were no longer any openings leading off to the sides.

The children came to a sudden stop as they ran into something solid. Taking a step back, they both screamed out of sheer terror! Hardly visible in the blackness, a face from a nightmare mocked cruelly at their fear. Strange horns twisted out from black temples, extending the width of the passageway. The fanged mouth opened wide enough to swallow them both.

For one long moment they stood there, petrified. Then a deep voice called, "There they are!"

The powerful beam passed over the children and lit up the demonic face. "It's just a statue!" Justin said shakily as he saw that the black depths of the open mouth formed yet another entryway.

He looked back. Short and Skinner were now running toward the twins, who stood unmoving in the glare of the flashlight. There was only one way open to them. Turning, the twins dove straight into the yawning blackness of the stone demon's open mouth.

Justin sensed instantly that this was not another tunnel. The sounds of their entry echoed against far walls as though they were in some great cathedral. They barely had time to step to one side of the entryway before the smugglers came after them, Skinner swearing as he banged his head against the low entrance. Then they caught their breath in awe as the heart of the great mound lit up for the first time in countless years.

The two smugglers did not even turn to look for Justin and Jenny, trapped in full view against the stone wall. Their attention was totally fixed on the treasures that lay before them.

"Hey, Short—look at all this!" Skinner exclaimed greedily, lifting the flashlight high. "That Spanish brat was right! We'll be set up for life!"

For a brief instant Justin and Jenny glimpsed a stone platform in the center of a high, vast chamber carved out of solid rock. The tightly bound figure of a man stretched out upon it, his withered features still preserved in the cold desert air of the high plain. His shrunken form glittered with silver and gold.

From perches high up on the stone walls, smaller gold versions of the stone demon that guarded the entrance glared down at the intruders, their jeweled eyes gleaming with a cold green light. Behind the funeral platform, the same strange figure that adorned the Gateway of the Sun shone down from an entryway identical to the one behind them. Stone chests heaped with the treasures of a lost civilization offered cold comfort to the long-dead ruler who would never again touch their shining splendor.

Justin and Jenny saw all this in a flash with their dazed eyes, then . . . *the light went out!*

"Skinner, what's going on?" demanded a high voice out of the darkness.

"I don't know! This blasted thing just quit on me!"

"How could it go out? That flashlight was new!"

"I don't like this!" Skinner grunted nervously.

"Don't be a fool!" Short snapped. "So the batteries burnt out. You brought an extra pair, didn't you?"

"Yeah, I forgot!" Skinner sounded relieved. Justin and Jenny heard a faint clinking as the big man replaced the batteries, then a deep, frightened voice growled, "Short, these ones don't work either! I really don't like this!"

"Hey, you aren't worried about that kid's story of the curse, are you?" Short asked . . . but his own voice was strained.

"I don't know, but this place spooks me! I'm getting out of here!"

"And leave all this gold behind? We'll be rich, Skinner!"

"Yeah," growled the big man, more calmly. "I guess you're right."

There was a pause, then Skinner added, "What about the kids? Are we just going to let them get away?"

"Forget the kids! They'll never find their way out!" Short said with finality. "Now grab some of that gold, and let's get going!"

Squeezed into the curved edges of the statue's backside, Justin and Jenny listened to the two men stumbling around in the darkness of the cavern. There was a muffled curse as someone banged a shin against something sharp.

The twins felt the warmth of a big body stumble by only inches away. Hoarse with fright, Skinner called, "Hey, Short— I can't find the gold! Or the entrance either!"

There was a crash, then Skinner cried out again, the words now muffled by distance. "Short, where are you? You've got to help me!"

Short's high voice answered faintly from somewhere far off. Frightened shouts echoed back and forth, each cry sounding farther and farther away. Then silence descended once more over the ancient tomb.

When the last cry had faded into the distance, Justin straightened up with relief. "I think its safe now for us to move out. Let's get out of here!"

He waited a moment, then added impatiently, "Well? Aren't you going to turn on the flashlight!"

"I can't get it to turn on!" Jenny answered desperately.

"What do you mean?" Justin demanded. He reached into the darkness and took the small flashlight from Jenny's unresisting grasp. He flicked the switch again and again, but nothing happened. He shook the flashlight. Something rattled loosely inside.

"It must have broken when I fell!" Jenny was crying softly. "Now we'll never get out! We'll be lost forever—just like all those other people who came in here!"

Sick with despair, Justin tossed the flashlight aside and slid to the floor. Without the pursuing glow of the smugglers' light, the darkness was absolute. It was a heavy, smothering blackness, so thick that Justin instinctively reached out as if to pull it away. But he couldn't even see the movement of his hand inches away from his face.

Jenny slid down beside him, and the two stared into the dark. Justin didn't know how long he sat there, arms wrapped around his knees, as his mind frantically rejected one idea after another.

"There's nothing we can do," he said at last. "We'll never find our way out alone."

Jenny sat up straight. She was no longer crying. "Yes, there is something we can do!" she answered firmly. "We can pray!"

Justin's despair lifted a little. "You're right, Jenny! We should have done that first."

He bowed his head. "Dear God, we're in real trouble! We'll never find our way out if You don't help us. Please show us what to do next."

"Please, God," Jenny echoed beside him. "We want to go home!"

The blackness around them didn't seem quite so heavy as they lifted their heads. *No matter what happens,* Justin thought, shoving his hands into his jacket pockets, *we aren't alone.*

One hand felt a hard object, and he jumped to his feet in sudden excitement. "My camera!"

He pulled the small camera from his pocket. "The flash will give us light!" he cried joyfully.

"But your batteries won't last the whole way back," Jenny responded.

"They won't have to," Justin answered confidently. "Just hold on to me tight!"

Jenny took a firm grip on the back of Justin's jacket. Justin felt for the rough edges of the carved entrance, then led the way through the stone mouth.

"There weren't any side tunnels here," he explained, "so we won't need any light."

Justin kept a hand firmly against one wall as they started back up the steep incline. It seemed a long time before his searching fingers felt emptiness. He stopped and took careful aim. "I don't remember which way we turned here. We'll have to use the flash."

He lifted the camera above his head. "Okay, here goes! Jenny, you watch for that mark."

He pressed the button, and a brilliant white light filled the tunnel, dazzling their eyes, then died away.

"Well, where's the mark?" Justin demanded.

"I didn't see it!" Jenny answered mournfully. "There wasn't time!"

Justin sighed. "We'll have to try again. I'll be looking

too."

He pressed the button again. This time Jenny cried out excitedly. "There it is! We have to go left!"

As they turned up the left tunnel, Jenny suddenly commented, "You know, I'm not even afraid anymore."

"Me either," Justin answered.

That peace and confidence stayed with them as they pressed onward. Each time they came to an opening, Justin pressed the flash. Often the flash revealed no mark, and the two children continued on past the opening. Other times, they discovered the little white marks that were their lifeline and turned in a new direction.

Several times the twins were sure they had lost their way, but always they came at last upon another of the telltale marks. The passageways continued to slope gradually upward, telling them they were heading in the right direction. Not once did they hear a sound besides their own soft footsteps. The smugglers seemed to be lost for good in the depths of the maze.

By now they had lost all sense of time. It could have been hours or even days since they had entered the *Cueva de la Inca Rey*. Occasionally they stopped for a brief rest, then pressed on, repeatedly placing one foot in front of the other until they were in a daze of exhaustion.

It was much later when Jenny pulled Justin to a halt after turning yet another corner. "Didn't the flash seem a lot dimmer that time?" she asked anxiously.

"I know!" Justin answered grimly. "The batteries are giving out!"

They turned twice more. As they stopped at still another junction, Justin raised the camera again and pressed the button, but this time there was no answering flash. He held the camera to his ear. There wasn't even the faint whirring of the charging flash.

Chapter 11

An Unexpected Reward

"It's no use!" he said at last. "The flash is dead." But somehow, even now, he wasn't afraid.

Jenny tugged on his jacket. "It doesn't matter!" she cried excitedly. "Look!"

Justin scanned the blackness. Then he saw what Jenny had seen—a faint gray glow far to their left.

"The entrance!" he exclaimed. "That must be the archway we came through!"

Their exhaustion forgotten, the two children broke into a run. Moments later, they burst through the stone archway near the entrance of the cave. All was as they had left it. The silver of the full moon still shone through the ruins of the shattered brick wall, turning the stone chamber into a place of quiet beauty.

But not for long. Before the twins had time to move, sirens filled the air, and the roar of a powerful engine screeched to a halt. The sound of running feet pounded below the battered wall.

Then a flashlight was thrust through the broken brick and the most welcome voice in the world called, "Justin! Jenny! Are you in there?"

"Uncle Pete!" The twins were through the archway and running in an instant. Quickly climbing over the pile of shattered brick, they threw themselves into Uncle Pete's arms. The sirens were silent now, but headlights from several vehicles lit the scene. And below, at the base of the mound, men in green uniforms hurried back and forth.

"Oh, Uncle Pete," Jenny choked out, her arms around his neck in a stranglehold, "I thought you'd never find us!"

His strong arms holding both children close, Uncle Pete cleared his throat several times before he could speak. "I was beginning to wonder myself. When I came back to the hotel and found you gone . . ."

His deep voice broke, and he hugged Justin and Jenny tighter, then let them go. "Come on! Let's get out of here."

Justin and Jenny scrambled down the hillside, Uncle Pete close behind. When they were once more on level ground, he hugged them again. "Okay, kids, what happened? Are you both okay? I know about the smugglers, so just tell me what happened tonight."

The twins' words tumbled over each other as they poured out their story. Already, the terror of the last hours was ebbing away.

"And the flash gave out just as we found the entrance!" Jenny finished dramatically.

"By the way, Uncle Pete, how did you ever find us?" Justin interrupted suddenly.

"I didn't," Uncle Pete answered with a smile. "It was Pedro here."

He turned around and pulled the Quechua boy forward.

Jenny and Justin had been so taken up with seeing their uncle again that they hadn't even noticed their friend standing patiently in the shadows.

Pedro's usually calm face was twisted with emotion, and the twins were surprised to see tears in the black eyes. "I thought you were all dead. I cannot believe that you have come out alive from the *Cueva de la Inca Rey*, but my eyes tell me it is so. I . . . I am so glad you are safe."

Justin reached out and gripped the other boy's hand. Jenny threw her arms around Pedro's neck and gave him a kiss on the cheek.

"You found us! Pedro, you're wonderful!" she exclaimed. A blush colored Pedro's high cheekbones, but his cheeky grin broke through the tears, and he hugged her back.

"You never said how you found us," Justin reminded impatiently.

Uncle Pete leaned back and crossed his long legs. "Well it's like this. When I got back to the hotel and found you gone, I checked with our American neighbors . . ."

"Yeah, we know! We heard you," Jenny interrupted. "We were locked in the bathroom."

"I know that now," Uncle Pete continued. "Anyway, I wasn't too happy about you taking off like that. In fact, if I'd caught you then, I'd have disciplined you good—thirteen years old or not. I checked around the market, but you weren't there, of course.

"Then I thought Pedro might know where you'd gone. I called Mr. Evans, and we drove up to the room he and his mother rent across town. He said he had no idea where you were. He was very worried when he heard you were missing. That's when he told us about your run-in with the smugglers."

He fastened a stern eye on them. "Why didn't you tell me

about this before, kids?"

Squaring his shoulders, Justin stepped forward. "I'm afraid that was my fault, Uncle Pete. I thought you'd laugh at us . . ."

Justin attempted to apologize, but Uncle Pete ruffled his hair and said, "You're forgiven, Justin. But next time, please trust me.

"Anyway, we knew enough then to search their hotel room. We found the gag and rope they tied you up with on the bathroom floor. Then Pedro found . . . Well, I'll let him tell the rest."

Pedro pulled a small, sharp object from his pocket. Justin looked at it in surprise. He had forgotten about the piece of pottery. "We look all over the room. Then I find this under the mattress. That is a very smart thing to do. I remember you showing it to the guard, and I remember the digging you told me of. I think, *they are telling us that the men take them to Tiawanaku.*"

Uncle Pete continued that narrative. "So we headed straight over to the embassy and got them out of bed. They called out the local police force—actually, their version of the National Guard. With you missing and the embassy behind us, they had to act."

He waved his arm toward the vehicles and activity surrounding them. "It took several hours to get things rolling. All the time I was afraid we'd be too late!"

For the first time since they had crawled out of the mound, Justin looked over his surroundings. A police car with red and blue flashing lights sat a few yards away. Beside it stood an open army jeep and a canvas-topped transport truck, painted in camouflage-green. Armed soldiers stood at attention on either side of the entrance to the tomb.

Jenny looked puzzled. "But why didn't we hear you coming? We didn't hear a thing until you got here."

"No, the colonel didn't want to warn the smugglers, so he left the siren off until Pedro here spotted the broken wall and guessed you were in the cave."

"*Señor!*" A tall man in a flashy, gold-braided uniform walked up to the group. Medals decorated his chest, and he walked with the bearing of a professional soldier. Justin guessed he must be the colonel. Mr. Evans and a short, over-weight young man followed him.

"Colonel Daniel Ramirez," Uncle Pete introduced. "And Mr. Appleby, an aide from the embassy . . . and Mr. Evans, of course."

The colonel bowed slightly. "I am pleased to see that you are safe," he said to the twins in perfect but slightly accented English. "We have found the vehicle of your kidnappers and the articles they stole. My men are now investigating the site of their excavation. Now, Mr. Parker, I would like to speak awhile with these children."

Under the colonel's skillful questioning, Justin and Jenny gave a full account of the events of the last few days—all but that brief glimpse of the ancient tomb. By mutual agreement, they had decided the treasure of the Inca Rey was safer left where it was.

When they finished, the colonel gestured toward the cave. "And you say these men are still in there?"

"As far as we know," Justin answered him.

"Are you sending soldiers in after them?" Jenny asked. Justin grinned to himself. His sister was obviously her normal inquistitive self again.

The colonel made the sign of a cross in the air. His hawk-like features were grim as he answered, "My men will not enter that evil place. I would not enter myself."

He studied the twins intently. "I still do not understand how it is that you have survived there alone."

"We weren't alone," Justin answered thoughtfully. "God was there with us." The colonel just nodded his head. He seemed to share Pedro's awe at seeing them alive.

"How will you catch the smugglers, then?" Justin inquired after a moment's silence.

"You need not preoccupy yourself," the colonel answered dryly. "My men will guard the entrance. If the *Americanos* come out, we will have them. If they do not . . . I think we need not worry ourselves about them again."

Jenny yawned, and the colonel's stern expression softened into a smile. He glanced at his watch. "*El aurora,* the dawn as you Americans say it, is not far away. Señor Parker, I do not think we need you any more tonight. You may take these two brave children home. But do not leave the city. I will need to speak with you further."

Jenny shuddered. "I don't think I could get to sleep in that hotel room—not without having nightmares. I'll think of those horrible men every time I see that place!"

Mr. Evans patted her shoulder. "Don't you worry. You aren't going back to the hotel. There are police all over the place anyway. You're coming to my place—that is, if you don't mind a sleeping bag."

"Oh, thank you, Mr. Evans. Thank you, too, uh . . . Colonel," Jenny said, holding her hand out to the colonel. Justin also thanked the colonel, and the tall officer strolled away, barking orders to his men.

"Isn't there someone else we need to thank, kids?" Uncle Pete asked, putting an arm around their shoulders. "Why don't we bow our heads before we go, and thank God for His protection."

For once Pedro had no scornful comment to make. He had listened with wide, unbelieving eyes as Justin and Jenny told of their adventures in the cave. Since then he had been strangely silent. Now he bowed his head with Mr. Evans and the Parkers as Uncle Pete prayed a short prayer of thanks.

The sun was directly overhead when the twins awoke on the hard, tiled floor of the babies' bedroom. The Evans babies had been carried into their parents' room several hours earlier. Justin was rubbing the sleep from his eyes when Mrs. Evans bustled in. Her round face twinkled with excitement.

"I'm glad to see you're finally awake!" she said with a smile. "You have visitors coming in half an hour."

She laid a pile of clothing on the babies' changing table. "Your uncle brought your things over from the hotel. I ironed a change of clothes for each of you. I hope they'll do. There's a pot of stew simmering on the back of the stove when you're ready."

The two children scrambled out of their sleeping bags. They'd slept in the clothes they wore the day before. Jenny pushed her curls back from her face. "Who's coming to see us? The police?"

Mrs. Evans' eyes sparkled. "Colonel Ramirez will be here and, believe it or not, the mayor of La Paz. I never thought I'd see the mayor in my home!"

She turned to leave the room. "Oh, by the way, you have another guest waiting downstairs for you now."

Justin and Jenny hurried into their fresh clothes and were downstairs five minutes later. Pedro was waiting for them when they entered the dining room. Mrs. Evans bustled in and set a steaming pot on the table.

"Here are bowls and silverware, so help yourselves. There's a pitcher of milk, too. I'll be in the kitchen if you need anything. I'm mixing a coffee cake for the mayor."

She left, and Justin turned to Pedro. Then he stopped, puzzled. There was something different about Pedro today, and he suddenly realized the defiance that usually showed even through Pedro's cheeky grin was gone.

"Pedro, what's happened?" he asked as he sat down.

Beaming with happiness, Pedro answered shyly, "I wanted to tell you that I have asked Jesus to come in and save my heart. Last night I asked Him."

"Pedro, that's wonderful!" the twins exclaimed together.

"I am sorry now that I laughed when you tell me about God," Pedro continued slowly. "I did know in my heart that the old gods were not good—that they were evil and cruel.

"But I would not believe your words. I wanted no part of a God of weakness. When I saw you come out of the *Cueva de la Inca Rey*, and saw that the curse of the old gods had no power to touch you, then I believed. I knew that your loving God was truly strong to protect you, and I asked Him to be my God, too."

Pedro was interrupted as Uncle Pete strolled into the dining room. "Hi, kids. Are you ready? Your visitors have just arrived. Come on, now. You too, Pedro."

Jenny and Justin looked hungrily at the untouched pot of stew, but they obediently followed Uncle Pete into the spacious living room. Two men stood looking out the window. Justin recognized Colonel Ramirez at once. Beside him stood a short, slim, middle-aged man in a dark dress suit. Colonel Ramirez introduced him as the mayor of La Paz.

Justin was disappointed to find that the mayor of Bolivia's

capital city looked as ordinary as his friends' fathers back home, but Jenny was delighted when the mayor bowed over her hand in a most dignified way, and said in English, "I am enchanted to meet you, *señorita*." The twins later learned that many wealthy Bolivians spoke some English.

The mayor then shook hands with Justin. "You have done our country a great service, and I wish to thank you sincerely. Without your help, more of our great heritage would have been lost."

He turned to Pedro. "You, Pedro Gutierrez, are a true son of your country."

Pedro was speechless before one of the greatest men of his country, but he grinned proudly at Justin and Jenny.

The mayor held out a hand to the colonel, who handed him a small packet wrapped in silk cloth. "And now," he continued, "I would like to present each of you with a token of appreciation from our government."

Opening the packet, he presented each of the three children with a fine chain, from which hung a silver medal. Etched upon the medal was the national seal of Bolivia. A llama and a bundle of wheat were silhouetted against the towering Andes mountains in the center of the medal, with the Bolivian flag on each side, and a condor spreading his wings over the whole.

The mayor turned to Uncle Pete. "You must be very proud of these *sobrinos* of yours."

Embarrassed, the twins shifted their feet uneasily. The mayor's sharp eyes noticed their discomfort, and he waved his arm at the sofa. "Come, let us all sit down. Colonel Ramirez has much to say before we must go."

As they sat down, Mrs. Evans, beaming with pleasure, carried in a tea tray and the promised coffee cake. She allowed herself to be introduced to the mayor, who rose and bowed over her hand.

As she finished serving, Colonel Ramirez said abruptly, "We must go soon, so let us now come to business. I will tell you what we have come to know since last night."

"Did you catch Skinner and Short? Are they still alive?" Jenny asked eagerly.

The colonel frowned at the interruption. "Yes, we did catch the two *Americano* thieves."

A strange expression crossed his face. "It was a very strange thing. My men say that they stumbled out of the *Cueva* not two hours ago. My men would not go near them at first, being afraid of the curse. But the two thieves did not try to escape. They just sat on the ground, staring at nothing.

"When my men finally arrested the men and brought them to headquarters, it was found that they remembered nothing— not about the cave, nor the smuggling, not even their names. The police medical officer declares that they are like children."

Justin and Jenny met Pedro's black eyes in a significant shudder.

The colonel continued, "Even now the entrance to the *Cueva de la Inca Rey* is being bricked shut again. We had to pay double wages before anyone would approach the *Cueva*. Word has spread about the American smugglers, and the people are more than ever afraid of the curse of the Inca."

He eyed Justin and Jenny intently as he finished, "I am not superstitious myself, but . . . I, too, will stay away."

The mayor set down his empty plate and added, "We have sealed off the smugglers' house and their excavation. The excavation will be of great interest to our archeologists. In the house we have found further evidence of the smuggling operation. However, there has been no sign of the third man,

Pepe. Concerning the *Americanos*, it is doubtful now whether they will ever stand for trial."

Justin was pleased that Pepe had escaped. Pepe was a smuggler and a thief, but he and Jenny might not be alive now if it weren't for his help.

Colonel Ramirez and the mayor rose to their feet. "Now, if you will excuse us, there is much yet to do."

They shook hands all around again, then walked to the front door. At the door, the mayor turned to Justin and Jenny. "I have forgotten one thing. Please excuse me. There is a finder's reward for antiquities surrendered to our government. You two have earned this fee. Arrangements will be made before you go."

The twins looked at each other. They didn't need to say anything before nodding to each other in agreement. Justin spoke up, "Señor Mayor, we don't want the reward. The treasure would never have been found if it wasn't for Pedro. We would like the reward to go to him."

"You are sure about this? For such a great treasure it is a large sum of money."

Over Pedro's protests, Justin and Jenny insisted that was what they wanted. The mayor nodded abruptly. "If this is what you wish, it shall be done." Then the colonel and the mayor were gone.

▼▼▼

Hours later the Parkers and the Evanses gathered around the supper table. Pedro was there too, crowded between Justin and Jenny. The twins had to tell their story again from the beginning for Mrs. Evans.

Now that they were safe, the terror of the night before had

vanished from their minds, and only the excitement of their adventure remained. Mrs. Evans exclaimed with horror at their tale as she shoveled mashed banana into her twin babies' open mouths.

When Jenny and Justin had run out of words, Pedro and Uncle Pete told their side of the story. Mr. and Mrs. Evans were delighted when Pedro then told of how he had asked Jesus to be his Savior. The long and noisy meal finally at an end, Uncle Pete leaned back in his chair and announced, "I bought plane tickets this afternoon—for tomorrow."

His bombshell stopped the conversation in mid-sentence. With everyone's eyes on him, Uncle Pete continued, "We've had a wonderful visit, thanks to you, Bob and Sally—not to mention a lot of excitement we could have done without. But I'm afraid it's time to bring our visit to an end."

He looked down at Justin and Jenny. "When I found you two missing, I told myself that if . . . I mean, *when* I found you, I'd put you two on the first plane home."

The twins looked at each other in dismay and opened their mouths to protest. Uncle Pete held up his hand for silence. His green eyes twinkled as he added, "That's what I decided *yesterday*. But now you're back safe . . . and—well, I changed my mind.

"I checked in at our company office this morning. While I was there, I received a call from the head office in New York. We have an oil exploration unit in the Bolivian low-lands that seems to be having a bit of trouble. I agreed to look into the problem. What do you say, kids, to a trip to the jungle?"

The twins' eyes shone with excitement. Over Jenny's excited squeals, Justin exclaimed, "Jungle! You mean a real jungle, like in Tarzan? Where they have monkeys, and dug-out canoes, and . . . and giant snakes?"

Justin leaned back in his chair, a satisfied grin on his freckled face. The adventure of the Inca treasure might be over, but he had a feeling plenty more adventure lay ahead.

About the Author

Jeanette Windle grew up as a daughter of TEAM missionary parents. She has lived in six countries and is now in Bolivia, where her husband, Marty, serves as acting field director for Gospel Missionary Union. When in the States, they make their home in Seattle, Washington. She and Marty have four children.